TYING
THE *Knot*

TYING THE Knot

A NEWPORT LADIES BOOK CLUB NOVEL

Josi S. Kilpack, Annette Lyon, Heather B. Moore, Julie Wright

Covenant Communications, Inc.

Published by Covenant Communications, Inc.
American Fork, Utah

Printed in
First Printing: July 2014

20 19 18 17 16 15 14   10 9 8 7 6 5 4 3 2 1

ISBN-13: 978-1-62108-793-9

Dedicated to our loyal readers.
Thank you, thank you for reading this series
and for the many e-mails and conversations.

Your support means the world to us!

BOOKS IN THE NEWPORT LADIES BOOK CLUB SERIES

Set #1

Olivia—Julie Wright

Daisy—Josi S. Kilpack

Paige—Annette Lyon

Athena—Heather B. Moore

Set #2

Shannon's Hope—Josi S. Kilpack

Ruby's Secret—Heather B. Moore

Victoria's Promise—Julie Wright

Ilana's Wish—Annette Lyon

For ideas on hosting your own book club, suggestions for books and recipes, and information on how you can guest-write about your book club on our blog, please visit us at http://thenewportladiesbookclub. blogspot.com.

Chapter 1

ATHENA
SOMETHING OLD, SOMETHING NEW

ATHENA SET DOWN THE FIRST-EDITION copy of *Woman in White*, her gaze sliding back to her parents' house . . . well, what used to be their house. She hadn't been concentrating on the book anyway while sitting in her car; she was too keyed up. Thirty minutes before, she and her sister had signed the official papers to close the deal on their parents' home. The Realtor would be arriving anytime, and at Athena's request, she'd be able to walk through the house one more time before turning it over to the new owners.

The sun was just starting to settle behind the Costa Mesa neighborhood on the warm August night, and Athena thought it strange that she'd grown up in this home yet no longer had the key. It had been empty since she and her sister, Jackie, had delivered their father to a care center. And they'd cleaned it out in the ensuing weeks. Athena had taken over her father's care after her mother's death, but in only two short months, his Alzheimer's had rapidly progressed, and Athena was no longer able to manage his care on her own.

If it hadn't been for Jackie's insistence—and Grey's—Athena's stubbornness would have led to greater challenges than chasing her father down the road at 2:00 a.m. and incurring a few bruises when she tried to stop his antics, like digging up the flower bed.

A car pulled up behind her, and the engine shut off. Athena looked in her rearview mirror, expecting to see Mrs. Paulson climbing out of the Jeep. Then Athena remembered the Realtor didn't drive a Jeep, and the person climbing out was a man.

Her heart stuttered at the sight of Grey. *He didn't . . . He did.*

Athena had met Grey the fall before, and it had taken her a good three months to appreciate the man he was. Thankfully, he'd been patient and even a bit stubborn himself. A smile played on her lips as she climbed out of her car.

"What are you doing here?" she said as he strode over.

"Thought you might want some company." He stopped close to her, not near enough to touch, but Athena could practically feel the warmth of his skin. His hair was its slightly messy self, and his brown eyes were intent on hers, gauging her reaction. He glanced into her car. "I see you're reading the Wilkie Collins book."

Athena smiled. "It's great so far. I might even recommend it to the book-club ladies." Grey owned a used bookstore and had the habit of giving her first-edition copies. So far, she'd loved every book he'd given her.

With Grey here now, she realized how glad she was that he'd shown up. She'd planned on going through the house alone, as a sort of farewell, but now maybe it wouldn't be so daunting.

Her heart thudded, and she reached for his hand and interlaced her fingers with his. That was all it took for his other hand to slide around her waist and pull her toward him.

"You aren't mad I came?" he asked, his face dangerously close to hers.

"No." She inhaled his subtle cologne, letting the scent of him soothe her nerves.

"I'm not intruding?" He smiled his contagious smile.

Athena moved her hands to his chest. "Knock it off."

"Just checking," he said, lowering his head until his lips touched hers.

No matter how many times Grey kissed her, Athena still wasn't prepared for it. They'd been dating for several months now, saw each other almost every day, and still Athena felt like she was part of some other world when he kissed her.

Her hands slid around his neck, and she was just letting herself get lost in his kiss when a car came down the street and slowed in front of the house. She reluctantly drew away but realized it was probably for the better; she was feeling a bit light-headed as it was. Grey had that effect on her.

Athena threaded her fingers with Grey's once again and then turned to greet Cheryl Paulson as she climbed out of her car.

"Thanks for doing this," Athena said, walking toward her.

Cheryl smiled, her lipsticked mouth stretching over her veneered teeth. "No problem, hon." She led the way to the front door. "I'll unlock it now and would appreciate it if you would close up when you leave. I have another appointment to get to."

"Sure," Athena said, grateful the Realtor wouldn't be hovering.

Cheryl left, and Athena stepped through the front entrance, then flipped on the light. Grey came in behind her, staying quiet. First Athena walked into the living room. Her most recent memories there were of her dad watching television in his silent world. His easy chair and television were gone now. Marks were still on the carpet from where the furniture had stood. The walls were scarred with nail holes where pictures of her family had once hung.

Next Athena walked into the kitchen. Her eyes smarted at the thought of her mother spending hours laboring over wonderful meals. Her mother had loved to cook, but Athena had never appreciated all her mother had done until she was gone. A cupboard stood open, and Athena crossed the room to close it.

This was the same house she had grown up in, but it now felt empty, even of the memories it had once held. Grey leaned against the doorway, hands in his pockets. "Are you all right?" he asked in a soft voice.

Athena exhaled, wondering if she'd ever truly be all right. "It's strange, you know? I guess I never thought things would really change. Time has a way of moving on whether you're ready or not."

Grey nodded, his gaze focused on her.

"I mean, look at all of this." She glanced about the empty kitchen; the white tiled floor was spotless, just like her mother had kept it. "Last year at this time it was a bustling kitchen—my mom was alive, my dad was home, my sister was trying to set me up on blind dates . . . and I came and went, not even appreciating what I had in my family." Her voice trembled, and she turned away from Grey, not wanting him to see her threatening tears.

He was across the room in seconds, wrapping her in his arms. "Hey, it's okay."

"I'm sorry. I didn't mean to get this way."

"Don't apologize," Grey said.

Athena closed her eyes, breathing him in. This man was remarkable. How had she lived all of her thirty-two years without him? He'd helped her take care of her dad during the most difficult times and had made her realize that keeping people at arm's length was stripping away the joy she could find in life.

"I'm glad time eventually brought us together," he said, pulling away.

"Me too," she whispered. When Grey got this serious, it created a nervous flutter in Athena's stomach. He was so much more open with his feelings than she was, and although she returned those same feelings, it was hard for her to be vocal about them after so many years of avoiding any commitments with men.

She knew she loved Grey, and he wasn't shy about saying he loved her. She met his gaze and let the warmth in his eyes spread through her body and cocoon her heart. One thing was for certain: she didn't know what she would have done without him for the past several months. It was like Grey had come into her life right when she needed him most.

Athena grasped his hand. "Let's go see the rest of the house," she said, leading him down the hall. They stopped at her parents' bedroom and flipped on the light. The carpet stretched against the blank walls. The bed was gone, as were the dresser, clothes, and bookcase. At least the curtains had been left—but the sight of them pierced Athena's heart. The soft drapes of pale blue had been sewn by her mother.

Athena noticed a white mound in the corner of the room, just below the drapes. Maybe a sock left behind? She released Grey's hand and crossed to the object, then picked up a lace sachet. Bringing it to her nose, Athena already knew what it would smell like. Gardenia. But she wasn't prepared for the way it overpowered her senses and clutched her heart. Tears stung her eyes. Her mother always kept sachets in her drawers . . . such a small detail to remember, but so much like her mother.

And now her mother was gone, and out of the entire house that she'd spent her married life in, the only personal thing remaining inside was this small sachet. Athena closed her eyes for a second, inhaling again. When her own life was over, what would she leave behind?

An empty home? A sachet? A lifetime of memories? And who would remember it? Her father's illness prevented him from even remembering her name. There was her sister, Jackie, who had three kids. The women of the Newport Ladies Book Club had become her dearest friends—at least the only real friends she counted. And then there was Grey.

Athena turned to look at him. He was there, like always, leaning against the wall as he waited for her. It was some cruel bit of fate that when she finally found a man she wanted to be with forever, her mother had already died and her father was too far lost to ever know him.

Her throat hitched as she realized what she had admitted to herself— that she wanted to be with Grey . . . forever. However long that might last. She crossed to him, and he straightened as she approached, his gaze a bit wary. Athena smiled to herself. She tended to be somewhat unpredictable at times, which probably explained Grey's reaction.

It was time to tell him exactly how she felt. It was time to stop wasting precious moments. She held out the sachet. "This was my mother's; it still smells like her." Her voice trembled, but not because of missing her mother—at least not entirely. It was because of what she was about to tell Grey. Something they'd talked about, but something she kept telling him she wasn't ready for.

He took the sachet and smelled it. "Beautiful." The way he was looking at her told Athena that he implied a lot more than just the scent of gardenia. When he handed it back to her, their fingers brushed.

Athena took a step closer and raised her hand to touch his face; then she moved her hand behind his neck as she lifted up on her toes. "I have something to tell you, Grey," she said.

"That you love me?"

She smiled. "It's more than that. I think I'm ready to move forward. To maybe look at rings." Then she kissed him.

Grey had no trouble pulling her tightly against him and kissing her back.

When she broke away from the kiss, he was grinning. "Are you finally saying what I think you are?" he asked.

Athena felt every part of her face and neck go red. Now they were going to *discuss* it? "Yes," she said, still breathless from what she'd finally told him and the way he'd kissed her.

"That's good, because . . ." he started to say, releasing her and grabbing her hand. He led her down the hall, back to the empty living room. "I don't want to wait even a minute longer."

Athena raised a brow, her heart pounding, as they stood in the middle of the front room. "*Now?*"

Still holding her hand, he reached into his pocket.

All possibility of catching her breath disappeared when Grey held out a ring—a diamond ring.

"Grey—"

"Don't interrupt me when I'm trying to propose."

Normally, Athena would have laughed at his comment, but her pulse went into overdrive, and her head felt light. This couldn't be happening. He had a ring already . . . He'd been carrying it. How was that possible? But as Grey knelt down and looked up at her, she realized it *was* possible.

She covered her mouth with her hand.

"Athena, you know how I feel about you, and you know how I told you I'd never ask you to change a thing about yourself for me," he said, looking straight at her. "But I've changed my mind. I want you to change your marital status."

Athena stared at the ring he was holding. The diamond was like the flame of a campfire—mesmerizing. She couldn't look away from it. That single piece of jewelry represented everything she'd avoided since she was a young woman and first felt the demands of fulfilling the traditional role of becoming a wife. She had wanted to be her own woman, not simply an appendage to someone else, and yet seeing the ring now made those earlier goals feel not quite so important. It was the crowning pinnacle of commitment she'd always feared would happen if she let herself actually be in a relationship with a man, to possibly fall in love.

And she was in love now. With Grey. She blinked back the moisture in her eyes. Was it really so awful? She'd never been so miserable yet so happy at the same time as she had over the past several months with Grey at her side, going through the pain and then finally through the quiet acceptance of her mother's death and her father's decline.

"Marry me," he said, his eyes searching hers. "Be my wife."

She didn't know what to say. She loved him, and she'd figured they'd spend a while looking for rings, might get engaged in a few months . . . But *now*? It all felt so fast. Wasn't it fast?

Grey stood and cradled her face with both hands. "If you need more time, I understand."

That didn't make her feel any less conflicted, and the disappointment was plain in his eyes. It was so Grey to say that—to not pressure her, to give her time. Her gaze moved past him to the empty room. Athena didn't want her life to be empty. She'd already lost too much. She didn't want to regret living another year, or even another minute, without what—or who—was the most important to her.

"I don't need more time," she whispered. "I want to marry you, Grey."

His eyes widened for a second, then a grin split his face. Before she knew it, he'd grabbed her into a hug and lifted her off the ground. She nestled her face against his neck, clinging to him—this man who was safe and loving and who argued with her and who kissed her until she couldn't breathe. And who was still holding her above the floor.

"Put me down," Athena said with a laugh. She couldn't believe it . . . she was engaged.

Grey lowered her to the ground but didn't release her. After kissing her thoroughly, he slipped the ring on her finger.

"It fits," Athena said, holding up her hand to examine the sparkling solitaire, tingles running through her body as she tried to process what had just happened.

"Of course it does," Grey said with a smile.

"Jackie told you my ring size?"

Grey nodded.

"And she kept quiet about this?"

He laughed. "It was hard . . . and I was getting tired of her texts asking for updates."

"I can imagine," Athena said, looking at the ring again. The diamond was elegant and strong above the silver band. "It's beautiful."

"I'm glad you like it." Grey tipped her chin up and brushed his lips against hers. "I love you."

"Mmm. And I love you, Grey Ronning." She wrapped her arms around his neck. "How long should we wait before telling Jackie?"

"Until tomorrow?"

"She'd never forgive me," Athena said. "You don't know Greek women."

Grey chuckled. "I think I know one pretty well."

The room didn't feel so empty anymore. "My sister will want all the details, and she'll have a million questions."

His hands trailed down her back. "Like what?"

Athena gave a small shrug. "Her first question will be 'When's the day?'"

"I'm open next week," Grey said with a wink.

Next week? Athena flushed at the thought. Of course he was kidding. "It will take me a lot longer to get ready than that. You know I hate shopping; it will take forever to find a dress."

He rested his forehead against hers and whispered, "So two weeks?"

"No—" Athena started to say but was cut off by another kiss.

When Grey drew away, he said, "I don't see why we'd have to wait."

Because . . .

Something she saw in his eyes made her want to get married sooner than later as well. But somewhere in the back of her mind she thought of her mother. What would her mother say? What would she plan for this long-awaited event? "There are tons of arrangements to be made. Invitations . . . all kinds of stuff."

Grey was watching her as if he didn't buy that they couldn't show up at a justice of the peace the next morning and get married. "All kinds of stuff, huh? So what would be your dream wedding?"

Athena lifted her shoulder, tilting her head to one side as she studied the man she'd just agreed to marry. She realized she didn't really care where they got married. She'd never been one to look through bridal magazines or visit wedding expos. "Anyplace with you."

Grey's smile flooded into her heart. "Okay, you got me as the groom. Now what's your dream wedding?"

Athena laughed. Was he serious? She'd never thought much about it, if at all. What was there to plan about a wedding? The church, a wedding dress, a bunch of flowers . . . She did know one thing—she wanted her family and friends there. As many of them as possible. Which would be impossible, of course. Most of her extended relatives lived in Greece, and all of her friends lived in California. There was no way to be in two places at once.

She stepped out of his arms and walked around the room as if the blank walls could give her inspiration.

"What are you thinking?" Grey said. "And don't say *nothing*."

"Well," Athena exhaled and looked over at him, "I guess if I had a dream wedding—it would include all my family and friends. But my relatives are in Greece. My sister and book-club friends . . . not to mention *you*, are here."

Grey nodded. "What are the chances of your relatives coming out for our wedding?"

The words *our wedding* sent a delicious shiver up her arms, and she folded them across her chest. "Nil," Athena said. "When they came for my mother's funeral, for most of them it was their first time to America—a once-in-a-lifetime trip."

Grey was watching her with a half smile.

"What?" Athena said.

"What if we got married in Greece? I'm sure Jackie would be up for it, and maybe some of your book-club friends could come—didn't Ruby and Gabriel say they wanted to go back soon?"

Athena stared at him, her heart thumping. He couldn't be serious. To go to Greece, where her heritage was, with Grey? Now that *would* be a dream, one she hadn't even considered a possibility. "They couldn't all afford to fly to Greece just for my wedding. I mean, how could I ask that of them?"

Grey didn't laugh, didn't argue, just looked thoughtful. "Maybe it wouldn't have to be only for the wedding. My brother did one of those

Mediterranean cruises a couple of years ago." He walked to where she was standing. "It could be a vacation for everyone. There are deals advertised all the time; I'm sure we could find one. Maybe Gabriel would have some good ideas."

"You're serious, aren't you?" Athena said.

"I'm always serious about you," Grey said, taking another step closer and placing his hands at her waist. "It wouldn't hurt to see what we can come up with."

Athena's heart fluttered; she didn't know if it was because of Grey's nearness or the thought of having a wedding in Greece. "All right," she said, thoughts spinning in her mind. First she agreed to marry him, and now this . . . "I guess I'd better call Jackie."

"Sounds good." Grey pulled her a little closer, his smile mischievous. "What about Ruby? Will you call her, or should I?"

Chapter 2
RUBY
MAKING A PLAN

RUBY'S HAND FLEW TO HER chest, warding off a possible heart attack, as she listened to Athena on the phone. First Athena had made the announcement that she was engaged to Grey—it was about time she scooped up that delightful man—and now she wanted Ruby to help her plan a wedding in *Greece*.

The news was so unexpected and wonderful that for a moment Ruby couldn't answer. Then it all came to her in a rush. "I'll plan on coming for sure, and I agree with Grey; if it were part of a cruise, it would make more sense for the other ladies to turn it into a vacation, and your sister Jackie needs a change of scenery from a house with those little tykes running around her all day. I'll have no problem letting her know a vacation is in order. Your own sister wouldn't want to miss your wedding."

Athena chuckled over the phone and said, "Thank you. I'm sure she'll appreciate the encouragement."

Ruby smiled, pleased that Athena had called her first. Well, almost first—after Jackie, of course. But Ruby knew even more than Jackie at this point, since Jackie didn't know about the location.

Moisture misted Ruby's eyes . . . this was like having a real daughter. Her daughter-in-law, Kara, was far off in Illinois, and besides, Ruby hadn't been involved in one speck of that wedding.

"I can call Gabriel if you give me his number," Athena continued.

Ruby's heart rate calmed as her impeccable organizational skills took over. "Don't worry about a thing, dear. I'll call him, and we'll put something together." Her mind raced over each of the book-club ladies. Shannon and her husband could afford the trip; they might even want to bring along their son, Landon. Daisy, Olivia, Ilana, and Victoria should be able to make it work as well. But there was no way Paige, with her two little boys and new divorce, could afford the cost of a cruise, no matter how sharp the discount. Ruby would have to see if Paige would let her help out.

"Thanks so much, Ruby," Athena was saying. "Work is crazy right now with the magazine, and whenever I have time to focus on wedding plans, Grey decides to distract me."

Ruby chuckled. To be young and in love sounded wonderful . . . although Ruby had quite her own love story going on. Warmth zinged through her at the thought of Gabriel. Dear, sweet, Gabriel. The man would move mountains for her, and after a disastrous, decades-long first marriage, Ruby realized not all men were created equal. There were still good ones to be found. "I'll call you soon, sweetie. Don't worry about a thing."

After hanging up with Athena, Ruby created a spreadsheet on her laptop. At age sixty-three, she was quite proud of her computer skills. In fact, her friends down at the senior center wanted her to teach a computer class. The thought made her smile. The idea of a "computer class" was so vague . . . It would be one thing to teach a class about spreadsheets, or using MS Word, or something a bit more specific. She could just imagine the lights dimming in the commons room at the center as she clicked through a PowerPoint. Snores would soon overtake the level of her voice.

The Excel spreadsheet loaded and saved under "Athena's Wedding in Greece" sent a jolt of satisfaction through Ruby. She rarely got to plan more than the monthly book-club meeting, which wasn't as easy as it seemed. There were many things to take into consideration, and Ruby had become adept at weighing all the pros and cons of a potentially tricky situation now that she knew each woman so well.

She typed "Shannon" on the first row, noting all of her earlier thoughts, followed by "Paige," adding to the cell: "Can't afford the cruise. Come up with a way to help Paige if she'll allow it." Next came "Victoria: Plenty of money between what they paid for her role in *Vows* and what she made on the sale of her screenplay. She should bring her new boyfriend, Christopher, along." Victoria would probably appreciate the escape from the paparazzi.

"Ilana: Has recovered well from her addiction. Greece will be the perfect vacation, especially if she brings that handsome doctor husband of hers. Olivia: This woman deserves a break, no matter the cost. Drag her on board if necessary. Daisy: New baby might be difficult to manage, but it would be a wonderful opportunity for her after dealing with that awful ex-husband of hers."

Ruby leaned back, satisfied with the list. Then she typed in her name as well. "Ruby: Make arrangements and offer to help pay for part of the cost. Explain it as a fabulous discount to the ladies."

There. It was all settled. Now she only had to call Gabriel.

He picked up on the second ring, and Ruby felt a thrill run through her at the sound of his deep voice. "Ruby, I'm glad you called," he said.

"You are?" She could hear his sister Maria talking in the background. He must be at the travel agency they co-owned. Ruby stood from the kitchen chair and walked into her living room, settling onto one of the white couches and digging her toes into the plush carpet. Talking to Gabriel made her want to settle in and get comfortable.

Besides, on the coffee table was a framed picture of the two of them taken in Greece only a few months ago. Now she could look at his handsome face and dark eyes as she talked to him. Ruby had gone on a two-week tour with her friends from the senior center, and Mr. Gabriel Alexakis had been the charming tour guide. The last thing Ruby had expected was to fall in love with him.

But here she was, and here Gabriel was . . . having returned from Greece and now living just a few miles away and working at the agency so he could be close to her.

"I hoped to confiscate some of your time tonight and take you out to dinner." Gabriel's voice came through the phone and seemed to wrap its way around her heart. How did he do that?

"I might need you earlier," Ruby said, wanting to relax into the conversation but knowing that a lot of people were depending on her— or at least they would be once they found out about Athena's wedding.

"I'm on my way," Gabriel said, his tone sounding quite pleased.

Ruby laughed. "Hold on. You don't even know my request. You're like a wild horse." She found herself blushing madly. Sometimes she said the darndest things around Gabriel without even thinking. She could picture his grin, which only made her heart race faster.

"I did do a stint in rodeo once."

"You did not," Ruby said.

Gabriel chuckled.

Ruby had to get off this topic, and fast. "It's Athena and Grey. They're engaged." She still felt breathless, and she realized that talking about a wedding to Gabriel might not be the best way to slow down her heart rate. "They want to look into the possibility of booking a Mediterranean cruise, one that stops over in Athens, and getting married there."

"Okay . . . wow."

"Yes, it will take some arranging," Ruby pressed on. "Especially since we're planning on inviting all of the book-club ladies and their significant others, and some of the children will probably come along as well. Oh, and Athena's sister and her family too."

"So a larger group? About how many do you estimate?" Gabriel asked, his tone business-like now.

Ruby ran the numbers in her head. "Thirty? I can't say for sure. If we have a couple of options laid out and different price points, we could firm up the number."

"What time frame are they looking at?"

"The sooner the better." Athena had hinted around three or four months out, but that might be the soonest a cruise could be booked anyway.

"This sounds like quite the event," Gabriel said. "I think it might take coming over to your house right away to discuss the details. I wouldn't want to leave out anything important."

"Gabriel!" Ruby said with a laugh. She noticed that Maria's voice had faded, and now Ruby heard a thud, like a car door shutting. "What are you doing?"

"Coming to see you," he said, his voice low, conspiratorial. "I really don't think we should delay any longer."

Her face went hot, and she wondered if she should turn on the air conditioner for the afternoon with Gabriel coming over. It wasn't often that she did, but his teasing made her feel a bit too warm. "All right, if you insist. See you soon."

She hung up and knew she had about sixteen minutes, maybe less, to make herself presentable. Even though she hadn't done any errands or gone to the senior center today, she never neglected her morning routine. She'd showered and dressed carefully as usual, but a touch-up would be needed.

She couldn't just shower and go like she could twenty years ago, but Ruby was able to make do quite well with the right products. She climbed the stairs to her main bathroom, passing her former master bedroom, now converted into a library. After her husband Phillip's death, she vowed never to sleep in that room again. And it wasn't because she was the grieving widow. It was because her husband had only been faithful for a few years of their thirty-odd-year marriage, and she didn't like to think of their marital bed or bedroom.

Looking in the bathroom mirror, Ruby dusted a bit of powder on her face, then touched up her lipstick. Raspberry-pink today, to match the raspberry- and white-striped blouse she wore with white capris. She fluffed her short hair so it framed her face, then sprayed a bit of hairspray. Her recent dye job added a few soft red highlights to the usual brown.

Ruby rinsed her hands to get rid of any makeup residue, and as a final touch, allowed herself one spritz of Pleasures . . . her new fragrance from Estée Lauder. By the time she got back downstairs and stationed herself as a lookout for Gabriel, he was just pulling up.

Ruby had given up on being shy or demure months ago, and as Gabriel climbed out of his car, she opened the front door to wait.

His olive skin contrasted with the pale yellow of his polo shirt, which was tucked neatly into khaki pants. For a man in his early sixties, Gabriel was an eye-catcher. Ruby guessed he could hold up to pretty much any younger man.

Gabriel's face broke into a smile as he spotted her on the porch. Ruby admired him as he approached, appreciating his height and the way his eyes held hers, never wavering. He didn't stop when he reached the porch but continued until he'd pulled her into a hug.

"I missed you," he said, his breath on her neck, which promptly sent a shiver along Ruby's back. Being in the arms of a man was a novelty to Ruby until she'd started dating Gabriel. She'd lived in the same house as her husband, but they'd been estranged for a long time as he'd indulged in affair after affair.

"I saw you not even twenty-four hours ago," Ruby said to Gabriel, wondering if any neighbors were peeking out their front windows to see her clinging to him.

"Too long," Gabriel said, pulling away. He gave her a light kiss, and Ruby knew he was refraining from a more passionate one. There would be plenty of time for *that* later. She had a cruise to plan.

But once they entered the house, shutting the door behind them, Gabriel had other plans in mind. This time, he kissed her quite adequately, and when she disentangled herself, she was glad she had freshened up. It made her feel more inclined to be romantic.

Feeling a bit light-headed and flustered, she said, "How are things at the office today?"

Gabriel ran his hand down her arm. "Great, once I got there. This morning was a bit rough since I had to unexpectedly meet with Rhea and then her psychiatrist."

Ruby grasped his hand and led him to the living room. "How did that go?"

Rhea was Gabriel's ex-wife. She'd been in a mental institution for most of the past year, and there was little hope of her making much of a recovery or living on her own. Her official diagnosis was termed *intermittent explosive disorder*. Rhea had tried to kill Gabriel more than once, and now the disease was progressing, leaving her in a dissociative or psychotic state more often than not.

Ruby's heart broke to know what Gabriel had endured in his marriage, and when he'd helped her get through the ghosts of her own past, it was the least she could do to help him in return. They sat on the couch, and Gabriel described the meeting with Rhea. His normally warm eyes went dull as he talked, and Ruby heard the strain in his voice.

"The new round of medications isn't helping," he said. "So they're going to ease back into the old ones."

"But they made her so agitated." Ruby had visited Rhea once, and it was the last time Gabriel had asked it of her. The meeting had turned into a violent episode, with Rhea panicking over Ruby's presence. Gabriel had thought it would dispel Rhea's notion that they'd get back together, but it had only sent the woman over the edge. Although Ruby had offered to go again to be supportive, she was grateful that Gabriel had turned her down.

Regardless of all the hurt Gabriel had experienced, Ruby hated to know his ex-wife was struggling. "What else can be done?" she asked.

"Nothing except for what they're already working on." Gabriel looked past her and exhaled. "Strides have been made in the mental health industry, but it's difficult to wait for better solutions when you know someone is suffering."

Ruby squeezed his hand. "You're remarkable to take on guardianship and oversee her care."

He lifted a shoulder and focused back on her. "You're the remarkable one. Always helping everyone else out . . ." His gaze warmed. "Now, what's this about planning a wedding?"

"Like I told you, the sooner the better, and it needs to be affordable," Ruby said, grateful to see her Gabriel returning to the present. "Is that too much to ask?"

"For anyone else, yes," Gabriel said, his eyes twinkling. "For *you*, no."

"All right, then," she said, standing and pulling him upward. "Let's get on the computer."

"I'm one step ahead of you for once," Gabriel said, fishing his phone out of his pocket. "I have a few contacts in Greece working on it now. Hopefully one will call back soon."

His phone rang as if on cue. Ruby laughed.

Gabriel followed her into the kitchen, answering it. "Peter! Did you find anything?"

Ruby couldn't quite make out the conversation on the other end, but judging by Gabriel's responses, it was all positive.

When he hung up, he grinned. "Ready for some good news?"

"Yes," she said, clasping her hands together. "Spill it."

"There was just a corporate cancellation on a seven-night eastern Mediterranean cruise in September."

"*September*? But that's only a month away."

Gabriel just kept smiling. "And you won't believe this. Peter can hook us up with the corporate rate, which is about half the normal fare . . . and the rooms all have balconies, which means they're the deluxe suites. Plenty of room for those who want to bring children along."

"Oh!" Ruby said. It was all wonderful. But *September*? She was thinking maybe November or even January or February. She refocused on Gabriel as he continued talking.

"We'll fly into Rome. The ports of call include the island of Crete, Ephesus in Turkey, Athens, and then back to Italy with a stop in Sicily, and finally returning to Rome."

"So the stop in Athens can be when the wedding is." Ruby hoped the stop would be long enough to hold a wedding . . . but she guessed they'd be in Athens a full day. "Can they accommodate everyone?"

"The booking was for forty-five, so there's plenty of wiggle room," Gabriel said.

Ruby took a deep breath. Maybe it was really going to happen, then. "And the price?" She braced herself.

"More than 50 percent off, with discounts for children. Of course, airfare would be extra." Gabriel paused. "But with my agency's discount, Maria can work some magic there too."

Ruby was nodding. It sounded like an excellent price. Even with discounts or special rates, she'd been thinking it would be at least double that. She could definitely cover Paige's expenses, if Paige would allow that. "Okay, let's see if Maria can get us an estimate, and then I can let Athena know what we're looking at."

While Gabriel talked on the phone with his sister and browsed airline websites, Ruby busied herself putting together a cranberry chicken salad. Gabriel had mentioned going out for dinner, but with everything going on, she preferred a quiet night at home. Her head was already spinning with all that had to be done, and adding the noise and commotion of a busy restaurant would just compound the chaos inside her head.

"Hold on," Gabriel said into the phone, turning to Ruby. "Round-trip flights will be about three hundred dollars less for each ticket with the agency package. One stop in Amsterdam, but it's the shortest flight routed. Just over fifteen hours. They can only hold the tickets for a few days at this price."

Ruby paused in her work. "That sounds good. I'll talk to Athena. Hopefully we can start booking in the next couple of days."

Gabriel spent a few minutes more on the phone with his sister, and Ruby turned back to dicing the boiled chicken. She always kept some on hand, cooked and then frozen, which made it easy to defrost in the microwave, then dice and throw into a salad.

With taxes and everything else, the cost per person would still be a fabulous deal for what was included, but it would still be way over some of the ladies' budgets. Paige's, for sure, and possibly Olivia's.

Then Ruby realized what she needed to do. If the offer was economical enough, then none of them could turn it down unless they were absolutely crazy or rushed to the ER the morning of departure. Ruby hadn't touched any of Phillip's investments, not in the two years since his death. She received online statements each month and knew there was a good stash, and that wasn't even in his 401k. She could help out whichever ladies needed it.

Ruby stirred mayonnaise in with the chicken bits, then washed her hands. Next she rinsed off some spinach. It would only take a phone call to her financial planner—which happened to be her neighbor—to liquidate one of the accounts. She did a quick calculation in her head. She could pay for everyone's airfare, and if she was remembering right, even the cruise. But how to present it to everyone so they'd accept it?

A pair of strong hands snaked around her waist, and Gabriel kissed her neck. "Did you hear what I said?"

"No," Ruby answered, leaning back into his arms. The salad could wait a couple of minutes.

"I said you don't have to go to all this trouble. I was planning on taking you out."

"It's all right," Ruby said as she reached for the towel to dry her hands. "We're not done planning yet. I still need your help with something."

"Anything."

Ruby turned in Gabriel's arms, facing him. "I want to pay for most, if not all, of the trip." His brows lifted, but Ruby pressed a finger to his lips before he could speak. "But no one can know. Ever." She ran her other hand up his chest. "Can I trust you to keep my secret?"

Gabriel was staring at her. "Do you think that's a good idea?"

Ruby hesitated a moment. She hadn't expected him to question her idea. "What do you mean? Why wouldn't it be a good idea to help them?"

"You know, I've watched you with these women—they love you and you love them back, but sometimes I think you try too hard to be a motherly figure and don't let yourself just be friends with them. They are grown women with families and lives and considerations. The cruise is already very discounted, the airfare is discounted too—it's an incredible price for them—and I wonder if you paying it down any more than that, making it a deal they don't feel they can refuse, is the right course."

Ruby saw what he meant, but she was also uncomfortable with the change of status he suggested. "Athena asked for my help."

"With the wedding—I know," Gabriel said with a nod and those soft eyes that reflected his compassion and sincerity. "But you don't have to make this happen for your friends, and if you did it in secret and they found out later, they might not appreciate it."

"I wouldn't want to upset anyone," Ruby said, frowning but seeing the wisdom of his words. "I know Paige can't afford it," she said, looking at him sharply—was this a loophole? "But she could use this trip as much as anyone."

"Then talk to her about it directly. Perhaps you can offer her a discount or maybe cover the costs and she can pay you back, but you've also told me how much pride she's taken in managing her little family these last months. Do you want to take the chance of her thinking you don't trust her to make this decision on her own?"

Ruby could feel the furrow between her eyebrows, and she looked away, knowing he was right but worried that if she didn't *make* this happen for all these dear women, it wouldn't happen. But was it fair to not be completely open with them? Even if it meant that they might not be able to come?

She exhaled in surrender.

Gabriel reached toward her and turned her face to look at him. In a husky voice, he said, "Did I ever tell you you're amazing?"

Ruby tried to look away, but he didn't let her.

"Your heart is as good and pure as any I've ever known," he said. "And I admire your compassion for these women, but let yourself be one of them instead of the ringleader this time."

She let herself relax . . . which always seemed to happen around Gabriel. He was right. "I think *you're* the one who's amazing."

Chapter 3

VICTORIA
THE TROUBLE WITH FAME

VICTORIA WORE SUNGLASSES—NOT THE cute little ones she loved with her whole soul but the ones that covered most of her face, ones like the big-time actresses wore in their efforts to avoid the camera flashes. Having always worked in the background on the hit television series *Vows*, she'd never had to worry about anyone recognizing her.

Until now.

Now she was wearing sunglasses and a big floppy hat. And she hated it.

"I can hear your teeth grinding," Chris said, giving her hand a squeeze as they walked through the farmer's market so she'd know he understood.

And he *did* understand.

Chris wasn't used to all the media attention either. Going out in public with sunglasses as big as their heads and hats that guaranteed they'd never feel the sun on their arms was uncharted territory for both of them. But ever since Christopher Caine, the hottest bachelor to ever grace the set of *Vows*, had changed the rules of reality television by proposing to *her*, the second assistant director, when he had been contracted to propose to one of the bachelorettes, the media had frothed into a madness Tori hadn't known existed.

She couldn't go grocery shopping without people pointing, staring, or taking pictures, or without other girls giving her the stink eye for "stealing" the bachelor right out from under the favorite bachelorette's nose. It was strange how so many people despised Tori for what they considered a backstab to Gemma when Gemma herself really hadn't minded all that much. She had been on the show for the payoff, and the studio had paid her a lot to walk away from the whole situation. Plus, Gemma had landed a role on a real TV series.

None of her fans cared that Gemma was thrilled with her current situation.

They still hated Tori.

Tori had never meant for any of it to happen. But now that it had, she wasn't sorry, even with the cameras, the fan mail and hate mail both, and strange requests for signatures as if she was famous.

She tightened her grip on Chris's hand and peeked at him from under the brim of her floppy hat. His olive complexion and dark features made him seem exotic. Tori couldn't blame all the women out there in the world. Chris Caine was a miraculous find.

No, she wasn't sorry. But definitely tired. And wanting time with Chris that belonged to *just them.*

"Know what I wish?" Chris asked as he added a guava fruit to her bag after paying the vendor at the fruit stand.

"World peace?" she answered with a smirk she wasn't sure he could see from behind her ridiculous glasses.

He grinned, his own big sunglasses looking so much better on him than hers did on her. "Forget the world. I'd settle for peace at a table for two. I wish we could get away to where no one knows us and be just us for a while."

It was as though he'd been reading her mind.

She wished the same thing five or six times every hour of every day.

A girl gasped from behind them, and then in a whisper that was really too loud to be a whisper, she said, "No way. It's Christopher Caine!"

Chris didn't flinch and pretended not to hear.

Tori had finally trained herself not to turn and gawk back, even though it was clear the girl *wanted* Chris to turn and look. For the first month after Chris had shocked Tori senseless by proposing to her instead of marrying Gemma on air, Tori couldn't help herself. When people whispered Chris's name or hers, she'd always turned to see who was talking. But she'd stopped turning when it became clear that *everyone* was talking about them.

It was all just so . . . surreal. She was Victoria Winters, the girl in the background, the girl who wrote scripts and loved to go purse shopping, the girl who hadn't had a meaningful relationship in her entire life.

Yet she held the hand of the most sighed-over man in all of America.

And he loved her.

Even better?

She loved him too.

She put a small tub of Bliss Farms raw honey in her bag and said, "It'll all die down soon. Once Max gets the most perfect wedding in history on film and shows it to the world, they'll get their fix and be on to next season's bachelor." She knew she sounded desperate with hope. Life would return to normal again, right? Her life would belong to her again someday, wouldn't it?

Chris let out a deep breath. "I hate the idea of getting married under someone else's direction. Takes all the romance out of it."

Tori loved Chris's Southern gentleman's accent. It thickened when he felt agitated, and he felt agitated anytime Max, the director, came up in conversation. She considered bringing Max up more often just so she could hear the accent, but she didn't give in to the temptation.

She understood Chris's feelings, but she still felt a great deal of obligation and gratitude toward Max. He'd been the one to allow Chris to propose to her, and for her to accept his proposal, without both of them getting sued by the studio for breach of contract. Max was also the one who had hand delivered her screenplay for a made-for-TV movie to Darren, where it had been green-lighted with the same studio that produced *Vows*. Her dream of being a real screenplay writer was coming to fruition.

Max had moved mountains and drained oceans for her.

And now she owed him her wedding day.

Chris insisted that dealing with Max was a little like shaking hands with the devil and trying not to get singed in the process. Tori had to be the mediator between the two men—Max, who felt like they should bow and offer to kiss his ring, and Chris, who couldn't understand how their lives had come under the ownership of Max in the first place. Chris was a self-made millionaire from the South. The only person in the world who bossed Christopher Caine around was his momma.

The girl who had uttered Chris's name a moment earlier trailed behind them with a friend who also gushed, but with more discretion—initially. She gushed about being a fan, about never missing one episode of *Vows*, about how she had even considered auditioning to be a bachelorette for one of the upcoming seasons. The girl grew louder and more annoying with every step.

"It really is him!" the girl gushed. "Hurry! Get your phone out. Take a picture!" They passed through a small courtyard to the other side of the market when the girl said, "I can't believe he's with that skank who stole him from Gemma. He totally should have dumped her by now."

Tori tensed. Great. A Gemma fan. Would the world never forgive her for undermining Gemma's place as the winning bachelorette? Tori considered the word *skank* pretty mild in comparison to lots of other words she hoped her mother never found out about that were used toward her these days.

Chris whirled around to the girls following them. "I would appreciate it if you didn't talk about my fiancée that way. We're real people with real feelings, and what you're doing shows an extreme lack of manners."

It shocked the girls to have Chris actually turn around and give them a lecture. They hung their heads and slinked away. Chris took Tori's hand and pulled her into a hug. "Let's elope," he whispered.

"We can't. We have contracts."

"We had contracts when we fell in love, but that didn't stop us."

Tori laughed and leaned into him, letting him brace her up and make her strong. Though she tried not to show it, the ugly comments from fans stung. "I sometimes think those kinds of people really believe they're talking to a TV and not to humans," she said into his shoulder.

"It'll all be over soon." He echoed her previous sentiment, the same desperate hope in his voice. "People will move on to somebody else's love life, since they'll never have one of their own."

"Let's go," Tori said. "Mom will be happy enough with what we got for the fruit salad."

Chris kissed her forehead and let her lead the way back to her car. She continued to use her car despite the fact that they could both afford flashier transportation. Her car and quasi-ghetto apartment made her feel grounded and normal.

The places Tori loved best were her car, Chris's car, either of their apartments, and her parents' house. The reason was simple: in any of those five locations, they could be relatively alone.

Except sometimes.

Sometimes the car became just another target.

She saw the word smeared on the windshield before Chris could jump in the way to block her view. It didn't matter what had been used to write the word. It might have been whipped cream or car paint or even spray paint. The method didn't matter as much as the word itself.

Not one of the nicer words. It made *skank* look almost like a kind greeting one would give to their grandmother.

Chris tried to stop Tori from marching forward. "Let me call a cab. I'll come back and fix this later."

"No. Let's just get out of here." The tremor in her voice proved she'd had enough. Someone had actually defaced her personal property.

Who did garbage like that? What kind of mental hospital escapee ran around insulting people by way of windshield?

"You're not steppin' one foot into that vehicle with that word starin' at you." Chris's accent had thickened so much it revealed his fury. He was a lot like her mom that way. The accents of their homelands swarmed them every time they lost control of their emotions.

Whenever he got that tone with that accent, Tori knew better than to argue. She sat on the curb to wait while he went off to fetch something to scrape and wash her windshield and then to complain to the complex manager about the vandals in their parking lot.

Once he'd gone, Tori stared at the car for several long moments. The whole world hated her for the simple act of her finding true love. How could a whole world be so cruel? She couldn't help herself.

She let the tears fall.

And fall.

And fall.

"Hey, there." A young woman said as she leaned over to peer at Tori. "Are you okay?"

Great. Caught bawling. "I'm fine," Tori said and took off her glasses to better wipe at her eyes.

"Holy—no way!" The girl who had been attempting to comfort a weeping stranger turned into a frothing fan before Tori even realized she'd taken off the only thing keeping her identity private.

Stupid, stupid sunglasses.

"You're Victoria Winters from *Vows*!"

Here it came—the moment the girl would start ranting about how Gemma deserved her moment to shine with her beautiful wedding and how Tori was an evil seductress.

"I totally love you!" the girl said, sitting down next to Tori on the curb as her brown ponytail bobbed with her excitement.

Tori blinked, unable to mask her surprise any better than she had her identity. "You what?"

This was new. No stranger had ever said that before. And even though the girl had plopped down beside Tori on the curb like an old friend instead of someone who didn't know her, Tori liked her immediately.

"It was so totally romantic how you two met and then tried to stay away from each other so you could protect each other . . ." She sighed and clasped her hands. "You guys are so perfect together." She sighed again, then straightened. "But wait. Is he why you're crying? Did he do something mean to you? I'll break his kneecaps for you if he did."

She looked earnest, ready to buy a baseball bat to club Christopher Caine for any wrong he might have done to Tori.

A stranger who didn't hate her.

Tori offered a very real smile to this angel in a world of demons. "I don't think I'll ever need to take you up on the kneecap breaking. Chris would never do anything to hurt me on purpose. He's actually left for a minute to . . ." She trailed off, unable to explain what Chris was actually doing without pointing out the car. "But thank you. You have no idea how much I really needed someone to be caring and *nice* for a change."

The girl looked a little bewildered as Tori leaned over and gave her a hug. "It's a bit unfair for you to know my name and me to not know yours," Tori said with a smile.

The girl returned the smile. "I'm Samantha."

"It's nice to meet you, Samantha." That was when Chris showed up with a security guard in tow. The guard carried a bucket that sloshed over with sudsy water. Apparently, Chris had talked the man into doing more than come out to write an incident report.

The woman saw Chris and about lost herself in a fan-girl swoon. She recovered quickly, though, when the events around her sank in. Chris pointed to the window, saying something that Tori sat too far away to hear. The guard nodded and looked apologetic.

"Oh, I see." Samantha looked back at Tori with a gaze filled with sympathy. "Thus the tears." She stood, walked to the car, and took the bucket from the guard. "Let me help," she said. She removed the scrub brush from the bucket and went to work on the windshield.

Tori stood as well and tried to take the brush from this stranger, but Samantha pulled away every time Tori reached for it.

"Some fans are crazy," Samantha said, her ponytail swaying as she worked. "And some are worse than crazy. My little sister is still in high school and is totally in love with One Direction. She's one of the rabid crazy. You two need to go find a tropical island to hole up on until the new season starts so you can get some peace."

"That's what I keep telling her," Chris said.

"It'll all blow over soon." Tori repeated this mantra three more times in her head while she kept her arms folded tightly over her chest and watched a stranger clean ugliness off her car. But she didn't know how much of her own words she believed anymore. The attacks suddenly felt so much more personal than they ever had before.

The words had been written with a latex paint. The water and scrubbing shredded the paint but not much else. The guard left and returned with an old paint scraper he'd found in the back of his supply room.

The scraper worked perfectly. Tori felt a degree of gratitude that it had only been the windshield. Not that her car was all that amazing, but she didn't want to scrape away her paint job.

She hugged Samantha again and thanked her for proving that sane, *nice* people still existed. Samantha asked if she could get a picture with Chris and Tori on her phone. Tori was only too happy to comply. The guard took the picture.

With the fiasco over, the guard and Samantha drifted away, and it was just Chris and Tori again.

Tori stared at the car, not wanting to get in.

"Let me drive." Chris took the keys from Tori. "It'll be okay."

She nodded and forced herself to be a big girl and get in the car.

They drove in silence all the way to her parents' house.

Her mom waited at the door, holding it open for them as they approached with their arms full of produce.

"What took so long?" her mom asked in her islander accent.

Though Tori's mom was *not* happy about the very public relationship of her daughter, she *was* happy to see Tori happy, and she genuinely liked Chris. Tori's dad wasn't nearly as annoyed by the publicity, since he really liked Chris as well. Tori didn't think her dad had ever approved of one of her boyfriends before, so this was a major breakthrough. The problem was that Tori's mom just didn't approve of the reality-TV method.

"Sorry, Mom. We were . . ." Tori shot a glance at Chris. "Sidetracked."

Her mom narrowed her eyes. "Is that your way of saying you were chased by news people and crazy fans again?"

Chris gave a tired smile. "Close enough." He pulled Tori's mom into a hug. "Not chased exactly. Just . . . bothered."

"That doesn't make me feel any better!" She accepted the hug but swatted him when he released her. "You keep those people away from my girl, you hear me?"

"I'm doing my best," Chris answered in earnest.

Tori smiled. Make that two people Chris took orders from: his momma *and* hers.

Tori took her turn to hug her mom. "He really is trying."

"I know it. I jes' wish, much as this hurts me to say, I wish you'd run away and get married where no one sees you—even if it means even I couldn't see you marry. This doing everything out where the whole world is watching feels wrong."

"See?" Chris said with a laugh. "Even your mom wants us to elope."

Tori rolled her eyes. Her mom was an intensely private person. Tori's new public life was hard for her mom to understand. "Contracts. We're not messing up any more contracts. We're lucky we haven't been sued for all the breaches so far. No more."

Chris and Tori's mom shared a look.

"I saw that! And I mean it." Tori took the fruit into the kitchen to start chopping it up for a salad.

"Don't you go getting angry with us, girl." Her mom followed her to the kitchen. "I jes' think you two need time for living normal. It's not healthy to be always looking over your shoulders. You need time alone where no one's watching you, no one's taking pictures."

"I know, Mom. I know." Tori's phone buzzed softly in her jeans pocket. She answered it and scooted aside so Chris could take over prepping the fruit.

"Hey, Ruby." Tori tried to wedge the phone between her shoulder and ear so she was free to help Chris, but her mom shooed her away, so Tori instead sat at the table, where her dad was setting the places.

Tori's face broke into a grin. "Athena's getting married?" Chris shot Tori a smile of approval at that news. He knew how much her book-club friends meant to her. Their good news was definitely Tori's good news too.

But then she stared at Chris with a look she felt certain he wouldn't be able to interpret. She listened as Ruby explained everything regarding the wedding details. Tori agreed to the plan with excited squeals and exclamations that had to make her sound like a ten-year-old at an amusement park.

She hung up.

And stared at her parents and Chris with a triumph and a relief she couldn't quite explain.

"What?" her dad asked.

"You be telling me what that wicked little grin means, bebe," her mom said.

Chris didn't ask her to explain. He simply waited.

"I think we have an answer to our need to get away from the press and be a real couple for a little while," she said.

"Which is?" her mother prompted.

"Athena's getting married," Tori said. "And we're invited."

"That's wonderful." Chris grinned. "But I don't see how—"

"In Athens. She's getting married in *Athens*. On a cruise to Greece. On a boat on the other side of the world, where no one will know us and we'll get seven days of peace."

Chris's grin widened as he whooped, picked her up—even with his hands still mucky from cutting up fruit—and spun her around.

Her parents looked relieved. Tori hadn't realized how much stress her new situation must have been causing them, and they didn't even know about the word painted on her car.

It would be only seven days away from the chaos.

But Greece . . . No one clicking pictures. No one whispering as she walked past.

No one painting cruelty on her car.

A break from all that had been building up would keep *her* from breaking. Ruby had just handed Tori a miracle.

A miracle on the other side of the world.

Greece.

Chapter 4
OLIVIA
A SMALL SACRIFICE

THE PHONE RANG. AND RANG. And rang. For the third time in as many minutes.

Olivia glared at it, her hands covered in flour water and soggy newspapers and her two daughters laughing as though there wasn't a ten-year difference in their ages. There was no way she had any intention of picking up the receiver. Why didn't the person just leave a message instead of calling back twice in a row?

Marie moved to get it, not caring that her hands were covered in a doughy paste, but Olivia said, "Ignore it, baby. If it's important they'll leave a message. We have a lot of piñatas to finish."

Marie acted as though the unanswered phone was a personal torture but went back to dipping her newspaper strip into the flour paste.

No messages were left the first two times the machine picked up. But after the third set of rings, the digital screen scrolled the words *message waiting*, indicating that whoever it was *had* finally left a message.

Mandy swiped goop on her younger sister's nose. Sometimes it was hard to believe that girl was seventeen.

Marie giggled and hurried to pat flour paste on Mandy's cheek, leaving a white handprint.

"War!" Mandy shouted and smeared little Marie's whole face.

Livvy shot a glance at the girls in their flour fight and then to the clock, gauging how much time she had before her husband came home from work. She felt a pang of panic for a brief moment—a need to hurry and clean the mess before Nick walked through the door and saw the kitchen buried in blown-up balloons covered in flour paste and shredded newspaper.

She forced her pulse to slow back down, forced herself to breathe and embrace the chaos—to let it exist so she could be *present*—not in fear of the future or worry over the past.

Those were the things the marriage counselor had been helping her work through. For Olivia, the repair of their marriage was all about relearning how to not feel the need to keep everything in order. For Nick, the counselor had been training him to be open about his feelings. Both of them still had a lot to learn in the way of communication.

But they *were* learning.

Which meant Livvy didn't need to frantically clean messes or yell at the kids to clean before the clock struck six anymore.

She smiled and felt a bit of heat creep up her neck at the thought of Nick coming home. There was something miraculous in knowing that he *would* come home. There would be no more waiting up and hoping and wondering. He showed up when he was supposed to and was happy to be with them.

So much to be glad about.

"Mom's thinking about Dad," Mandy said, pointing her gloppy finger at Livvy.

"How do you know?" Marie scraped her hand down her face in an effort to clean herself off.

"Goofy smiles. Whenever she gets her goofy smile, you know you don't want to be in the room when Dad comes home."

"Why not?" Marie asked, trying to figure out what her older sister knew that she didn't know.

Mandy dropped her voice to a low, conspiratorial whisper. "Because there will be kissing."

Marie groaned, stuck out her tongue, and made vomiting noises. But Mandy grinned instead of joining her younger sister in being grossed out by kissing parents. Having recently turned seventeen and having lived through the turbulent silence of her parents' relationship, Mandy had come to appreciate the beauty of kisses in a way Marie couldn't comprehend in her scant seven years.

Tyler, who'd gotten moody after hitting double digits in age, came into the kitchen to forage; saw the mess; stole a look at Mandy, who suddenly seemed interested in him as she swiped her hand through the bowl; and hurried to exit before Mandy could organize an attack.

"Dumb kid," Mandy muttered as she went back to running strips of newspaper into the bowl. "He wasn't supposed to leave yet."

"I think that makes him smart. He knew what you were up to," Marie said, always quick to defend her brother. She covered her bright pink balloon with a clumpy piece of paper.

Livvy didn't think Mandy would use any of the piñatas Marie had helped make, since they were pretty sloppy. But then . . . she might. Along with Nick and Livvy figuring out their marriage, the kids were also figuring out their relationships and places in the family.

The family had never been so strong.

It thrilled her.

And terrified her.

The newfound peace felt so fragile. Not just within her own little family unit of Nick, her, and their four kids, but with *all* of them. Nick had come so far in his efforts to include his two kids from his previous marriage and his grandkids in their lives that Livvy felt a stinging in her eyes just thinking about it. She chided herself for her fear of losing it all again.

She'd talked to the marriage counselor about this subject a lot—her fear of everything falling apart again. It had all been so ugly with Nick moving out and asking for a divorce because she'd pushed too hard to make him have relationships with his two kids, Kohl and Jessica, from his marriage to the Ex. Livvy's pushing too hard had backfired because she hadn't known that Nick harbored secrets that shamed him and cut into his proud core. It had been easier for him to walk away than to face his own truths.

The truth was that Kohl wasn't Nicholas Robbins's biological child. His ex-wife had cheated on him, and Kohl had been a result of that affair. Nick hadn't discovered Kohl's parentage until much later—after Nick had married Livvy and had two more kids. His realization that Kohl wasn't his had been the beginning of the spiral that had led the family into a jungle of noncommunication.

But things were better. Kohl and Nick were talking on the phone a lot, writing e-mails and physical letters back and forth, going to Lakers' games when Kohl was on leave, acting like a *family*. Nick had claimed Kohl as his own son whether they shared blood or not.

Livvy loved it.

And feared it going away.

Stop it, Livvy. Think glad thoughts.

So she turned her attention back to Mandy and the piñatas they were making for the back-to-school party Mandy was having that weekend. Livvy hated that the school year was starting already. Mandy would be a senior, and Chad had already left for college.

Things were changing.

Soon enough it would be just her and Nick in the house. That thought didn't scare her anymore. Part of her even looked forward to it.

That was a glad thought.

She worked alongside her girls, talking, laughing, and brainstorming different design ideas for each piñata until they were finished.

"I think we're done," Mandy said, surveying the drying papier-mâché. She washed her hands and turned to leave the kitchen when Livvy stopped her.

"Did you forget something?"

Mandy glanced at the messy countertops and dishes and groaned. "But I have homework."

"You also have housework. You do counters. I'll do dishes."

"What about Marie?" Mandy didn't mind throwing her sister under the bus when it came to chores.

"She gets floors," Livvy said loud enough to make certain the seven-year-old heard the command before she slipped out of the kitchen.

Marie let out a groan of her own but went to the closet to get the broom and mop.

Livvy smirked at the girls and cleared the dishes to the sink. There really weren't that many, and it only took a moment to load the dishwasher and clean her hands off. Since the girls were still cleaning, she decided to stay in the kitchen so they didn't feel like she'd abandoned ship on them. She went to the phone and listened to the messages.

Ruby's voice came on and filled the kitchen, which made Livvy smile and feel a little sad she'd ignored the call. Ruby had pretty much saved Livvy's life by starting the book club. Ruby likely didn't even know it. Livvy hadn't shared with anyone all that she'd been going through, but the steady presence of the women in her book club—along with the books they'd chosen to read—had given her the strength to stand on her own two feet again.

Ruby certainly sounded energetic in her message, pleading with Livvy to call back *immediately* because there was wonderful news to be shared.

"Someone in my book club is getting married," Livvy said to the girls as she dialed Ruby's number.

"How do you know?" Mandy asked.

"Because Ruby sounds a little manic."

Luckily, Ruby didn't answer until *after* Livvy had called her manic.

"I'm so glad you called back!" Ruby said.

"What's up?" Livvy had to lift one foot and then the other as Marie mopped under them.

"Athena's getting married!" Ruby said with a squeal that made Livvy smile.

"Wonderful!" She put her hand over the mouthpiece of the phone and whispered to her girls. "Yep. Married. It's Athena."

Mandy gave a thumbs-up from where she was washing down the front of the lower cupboards, where the drippings from their project had started to crust over.

Ruby went on. "You know how hard it is for Athena to not have her mom in her life and to have her dad mentally out of reach. She really wants family around her for this event, so she's decided to get married in Greece."

"Greece?" Livvy felt a little disappointed. She wouldn't be able to go. She hated the idea of missing her friend's wedding.

"Won't that be wonderful?"

Livvy felt genuine happiness for Athena in spite of feeling bad for her inability to be there for the event. "Absolutely wonderful. It's what her mother would have wanted."

"Exactly. But Athena also wants her dearest friends at the wedding. That's us. So she asked if I could ask Gabriel to pull some strings at the travel agency. He has some people who owe him some major favors for running tours he never got paid for. He scored us a deal that is so cheap it would be scandalous for us not to take it!"

Hope blossomed in Livvy's chest. A good deal on a trip to Greece might be the sort of thing she and Nick could manage. It would be a wonderful time to get away, just the two of them. The counselor said they needed to work on making time that was just for them as a couple. But time alone had proven hard to come by.

Ruby continued. "There was a cancellation on a cruise leaving from Rome that docks in Athens. The cruise is more than 50 percent off. But don't let the price fool you. I promise the cabins are the nice ones that overlook the water. We won't be sleeping with the engines. And Gabriel's sister managed to get a great fare on plane tickets. Kids under the age of twelve fly free with the promotion."

Livvy allowed herself to indulge in the idea of such a huge family vacation but dismissed the idea almost as quickly as it came. Nick and Livvy needed time *alone*.

"Just think of it!" Ruby said. "Rome, Crete, Ephesus, Athens, and Sicily! Think of the things we'll see and experience! Gabriel knowing the ins and outs of the travel industry is definitely going to be a perk to my friendship with him."

Livvy smiled at the denial Ruby had to be in if she was calling her relationship with Gabriel a friendship. Livvy knew fire when she saw it, and a flame burned steady in the hearts of Ruby and Gabriel for each other.

"So do you want to book passage for your kids too or just for you and Nick?" Ruby asked.

This was a wonderful opportunity. A deal too good to pass up.

Except . . .

A cruise.

A cruise was still a bit of a sore point in her marriage. Nick had tried to surprise her—a cruise planned during a time when she had organized a going-away party for Kohl before he deployed. Nick had chosen the cruise over his own son.

And that had made Livvy furious.

It was the first time Livvy had stood her ground with her husband, even if that ground felt like quicksand at the time.

They hadn't ended up going on a cruise.

They'd almost ended up divorced.

There was no way Livvy could bring up the subject of a cruise to Nick now, not when they were doing so well.

Nick was happy. She was happy. Their kids were happy. Things were good. She wanted them to stay that way.

She lowered her voice and turned away from her girls, wishing she hadn't insisted on a corded phone in the kitchen. If only cordless phones didn't get lost so easily. "Ruby . . . that is an amazing deal, a once-in-a-lifetime opportunity, but . . ." Livvy swallowed hard and searched for the right words. "I'm going to have to pass and let it be someone else's opportunity."

A stunned silence followed as Ruby processed Livvy's response. She braced herself for the questions she didn't know how to answer.

"Are you serious? You're saying no? But . . . but why?" Ruby sounded so desperately sad, as if she'd failed at something where she had felt sure she'd succeed.

"I'm sorry. I would love to be there. You know Athena means the world to me. You *all* mean the world to me. I just . . . can't." Livvy closed her eyes and tried not to feel the disappointment.

When she opened them again, Mandy had stopped cleaning and was frowning and staring at her with a look that meant Livvy would have to relive this conversation as soon as she hung up the phone.

"It's okay," Livvy mouthed, hoping to reassure her teenager.

And it *was* okay. If she had to choose between a cruise and family, family won every time.

She'd already made that choice once before.

"What's wrong?" Ruby asked. "What aren't you telling me?"

Marie had finished the floor, put the mop and broom away, and now hurried out before Livvy could assign any more chores. The girl had remained blissfully unaware of the tension that had suddenly constricted the atmosphere of the kitchen.

But Mandy hadn't been unaware, and though she'd left the kitchen with her sister, she would be asking questions later.

Livvy sighed, wishing Mandy hadn't been there to witness anything. The disappointment was enough for Livvy to deal with alone. She didn't want to share that disappointment with anyone. "I've had some struggles in my marriage." She couldn't believe how hard those words were to say out loud to anyone besides the counselor. She'd hoped she'd never have to say them to anyone else. But she owed Ruby an honest explanation. "Everything came to a breaking point when my husband dropped a surprise cruise in my lap last fall, and I . . . well, I refused to go. It's a long story. But the cruise is a sore point still."

Ruby let out a tiny gasp.

"But don't worry," Livvy hurried on to say, not wanting to incriminate Nick in any way. Something she'd learned after they'd gone to marriage counseling was how much her husband appreciated that Livvy had never publically bad-mouthed him. He said that her always speaking well of him made him want to rise to the occasion and prove her right. He said her behavioral quirk—knowing she would only speak the best of him—had allowed him to feel safe in trying to come back and fix his mistakes. She'd acted that way out of instinct. Speaking well of people was simply her way.

Now that she knew the result of her previous actions, she remained vigilant in keeping them up. "Everything has been getting better. We're working very hard to make things good for everyone in the family. But I don't think Nick would appreciate me throwing a cruise into the works when I refused to go on one with him. My husband's pride is a big deal. No. Not pride . . . his self-worth. I don't want to bruise his emotions. I want to be careful."

Livvy rubbed a hand over her eyes. She knew her explanation lacked any intelligible information, but she couldn't make anything come out right. "I love my family and simply want to do the right thing by them. You understand, don't you?"

Another painful silence followed before Ruby answered, "Of course I understand. I just feel terrible you kept all that to yourself when we could've helped you. If nothing else, I could have been a listening ear."

"I know. But believe me; you *were* there for me . . . more than you can ever know. Anyway, I am so excited for Athena. I'll explain everything to her, but you guys had better take tons of pictures for me so I can live it all vicariously when you get back. I love you. Thanks for inviting me."

After a few more parting salutations and declarations of Ruby wishing Livvy could be there, they hung up.

Mandy entered the kitchen again before the phone could be put back on the cradle.

"What?" Livvy asked after a minute trying to figure out how much her daughter had heard or if she'd heard all of it.

"Sooo . . . that was an interesting conversation."

"I thought you were doing homework?"

Mandy shrugged. Mandy and Livvy had all kinds of open conversations. Theirs was a no-holding-back-anything kind of mother-daughter relationship, for better or for worse. It was how they'd always been.

"Athena's getting married in Greece. Ruby's boyfriend, Gabriel, managed to swing some pretty amazing deals on flights and cruise fares. Fares so good they're almost unbelievable. But . . ." Livvy frowned and sat with a sigh on one of the barstools.

"You told them no."

Livvy nodded. "It's the best choice."

"It's a dumb choice. You should go."

"Yeah, Manda-bear. I'll just tell your dad that I've got a surprise cruise I want him to go on with me, even though I refused to go on the surprise cruise he sprang on me. Do you have any idea how much that would hurt him?"

"Hurt-schmurt. Dad would probably want to go too."

Livvy rested her elbows on the counter. "It's complicated," she said, not wanting to burden her daughter with the complexities. "We're in a good place, and I want to focus on the future, not get stuck in something hard from our past."

Mandy shook her head. "Unbelievable. Why are you going to counseling if you're not going to talk about something like this with Dad before you decide for him?"

"Mandy . . ." Livvy used her mommy-warning tone like she had when the kids were all little.

"Mom . . ." Mandy rolled her eyes and mimicked the tone. "Just talk to him. Tell him about this great deal, and tell him you want to go away with him so you can smooch his face off without the kids getting grossed out."

Livvy laughed. "I'll think about it."

"Which is mom-code for, 'I'm saying this to shut you up but have no intention of pursuing this any further.' Right?"

"You're impossible." Livvy grabbed the dishrag Mandy had abandoned on the island and got up to rinse it in the sink. She didn't deny the truth in Mandy's words. Mandy made some sort of *psh* noise at her and went off to her room to hopefully do the homework she'd insisted she had.

Livvy made a second round of wiping the dishrag over the counters. Not because they needed it but because she needed to think.

Sadness took little nibbles at the edges of her happiness. A cruise would be so much fun. Nick had always talked about taking her on one. And to Greece? For a third the cost of a cruise ship leaving Los Angeles? "I just might be an idiot for turning this one down," she said to herself.

She had moved back to the sink to rinse the rag again when strong arms were suddenly on either side of her, caging her in. She knew those arms.

"Who's an idiot?" Nick's voice whispered in her ear. "Certainly not my Livvy."

"Welcome home, babe," she said as he dropped a slow, lingering kiss at the nape of her neck.

Shivers coursed through her whole body. Dang, but that man knew how to kiss her.

"Why are you calling yourself names while scrubbing an already clean sink?" he asked.

She almost gave in and told him. She really wanted to, but mentioning the cruise could undermine all they'd worked toward these last several months. Not worth it. She turned in his arms to look at him directly.

Her legs almost buckled at the smolder she saw in those eyes. She would never get tired of knowing how much he loved her. She made her choice right then and there as she looked into the face of the one person on the planet she would never get enough of. She leaned in to get to some of that kissing her daughters pretended to be so grossed out by. Who needed a cruise?

She had her husband. Such a small sacrifice for so great a man.

Chapter 5

VICTORIA
CHANGE OF PLANS

TORI COULDN'T BELIEVE HER LUCK. A cruise vacation away from the world! After the experience with the car, she knew she needed time away or she would crack entirely. She looked at Chris as he drove her home from her parents' house and smiled to herself. *Lucky me*, she thought.

"What are you grinning at?" Chris asked, having caught her smiling at him.

"At how lucky I am to have you."

"You might not think that when I leave my socks in the middle of the floor."

"Sure I will. I'll think it the whole time I scold you and make you pick up after yourself."

He laughed and made the turn onto her street. After he parked out front, she waited until he came around to open her door and hand her out of the car—an act he insisted any man raised properly would do. She'd long since stopped arguing the issue and just enjoyed that he was a gentleman at all times.

With her hand in his, they meandered up her front walk, leaning into each other and slowing their pace with each step since neither of them enjoyed this part—the good-bye part.

At the doorstep to her apartment, he turned to her and took her face in his hands. "Soon," he said.

"Soon," she repeated, meaning that soon they wouldn't have to do the good-bye part. He leaned in and pressed his lips against hers for a long kiss good night.

A voice came from behind them. "Sorry to intrude!"

They split apart and frantically turned to face the person who had indeed intruded no matter what she said she was sorry for. "Mrs. Saxton," Tori said as politely as she could. "What are you doing?"

Mrs. Saxton had always been a poke-around-in-other-people's-business kind of neighbor, but since Tori had become "famous" due to becoming engaged to Christopher Caine, the nosiness had really gotten out of hand.

"I wanted to make sure you got your mail. The postman was just going to leave it in front of your door since the package didn't fit in the box, but I told him I didn't mind taking the burden of responsibility and making sure you received it in person. I mean, we wouldn't want that now, would we? Imagine! Leaving your mail out in the open for anyone to poke around in! I told him that was seriously unprofessional of him."

Chris had widened eyes and a smile of disbelief on his face as Mrs. Saxton blabbered on and on, her toes drumming against her rainbow-striped flip-flops. Tori knew what Chris's look of bewilderment was saying: *Doesn't she realize she just ruined a perfectly good kiss?*

Of course Mrs. Saxton *knew*, which was why she stood out there on the front step at that exact moment.

Tori held out her hand to try to put a stop to the endless stream of words exiting Mrs. Saxton's mouth. "Thank you for your courtesy, but it's so much easier for me if my mail is left by my door. I can get it on my way into my apartment that way. But since you've got it, I'll go ahead and take it in now."

Mrs. Saxton looked confused a moment before she said, "Oh, right! I left it in my apartment in case it wasn't you out here. I'll be back in a tick." She shuffled away, her flip-flops hindering any actual hurrying.

"Of course she doesn't have it with her." Chris grumbled low enough to be sure only Tori heard him. "Because who else would be out here making out in front of your door?"

"We were not making out!" Tori insisted.

He grinned. "Not yet . . ."

She laughed and was about to respond when Mrs. Saxton returned with a pile of mail. Tori took the pile from Mrs. Saxton's hands and thanked her, though she didn't feel all that grateful. She was definitely not going to miss this lady when she moved away.

"You get quite a lot of fan mail, don't you?" Mrs. Saxton asked.

Tori smiled at Mrs. Saxton instead of responding, opened her door, and let Chris inside so they could say good-bye in private. "Thanks again!" Tori said and shut the door before Mrs. Saxton could say anything else.

She leaned against the door in relief. Chris stepped in close. "Now, where were we?"

The small package on top of the envelope pile got in the way of where they were, so Tori walked over to the table to set it all down. She looked at the package wrapped in bright, cheery red mailing paper like a birthday present.

Max had told her he'd be sending some chocolates from France, where he was scouting out a location for the next season. She ripped off the paper and opened the box, figuring she could share with Chris.

"Seriously?" Chris asked. "You chose mail first?"

She frowned as she took the card from off the top and peered into the box at what was definitely not chocolate. "It's a clock," she said, trying to understand why her heart rate took a sudden jump at something so simple.

Chris leapt to her side and shoved her away from the box. He peered inside. "Someone sent you a bomb?" She'd never heard him sound like that, filled with terror and horror and everything in between.

Bomb. That was why her heart had stuttered at the sight of it. She'd made the mental connection without even realizing it. Chris kept himself between her and the box as he yanked his phone from his pocket and edged her back toward the door.

She still held the card tight in her fingers. She glanced down and saw the words written at the top, "You're dead if you go through with this wedding."

The world started to spin into a kaleidoscope of nauseating color.

"I need the police. I have an emergency," Chris said into his phone.

The police were at her apartment for a long time. The clock turned out to be only a clock and nothing more. Mrs. Saxton acted as though the attack had been made on her personally and fanned herself as though she might swoon. *Maybe that'll teach her to stay away from my mail,* Tori thought and then felt mean for thinking it.

Her neighbor's little yappy dog barked at the officers until the bomb squad captain, or whatever he was, ordered Mrs. Saxton to put that thing in her own apartment.

Once the circus of police, investigators, and bomb experts had finally declared the premises safe, they cleared out, leaving only Tori and Chris again. Afternoon had melted into evening, which now bordered on night.

"You should go home. You need to sleep," Tori said to Chris, who looked exhausted straight to his bones.

"I am not leaving you here alone."

She needed to sleep too but felt guilty for going to bed when he refused to do any such thing. He insisted on staying awake. He ultimately won the argument when he reminded her that whatever sicko had sent the package had her address. They could come at any time. And Chris wasn't about to sleep through that.

Tori was too tired to talk him out of it. She got him a pillow and blanket in case he decided to take a nap on the couch. Secretly, she was glad he stayed. She doubted that any amount of exhaustion would have driven out the fear of that stupid clock.

She'd had death threats before. The first had come almost immediately after Chris's proposal to her had aired. The fact that someone was so passionately against Chris and her being together that they were willing to graphically describe how they planned to end her life had certainly kept her up several nights in a row. Max had assured her that crazy letters were normal. Apparently, everyone got them. He told her not to worry about it because the studio would take precautions to keep her safe.

Tori had learned to live with the letters and e-mails, both the good ones and the psycho ones. But this felt different. This person had written about dates and locations that proved they had insider information in regard to the wedding. It made her tremble with a visceral fear. She was grateful to lose herself in sleep.

The next morning she woke to find that the blanket was still folded on the couch with the pillow on top—obviously untouched. Chris was at the table with her laptop.

"You didn't sleep at all?" she asked, feeling guilty that she had slept pretty well once she'd been able to relax.

He stood and crossed the room to her. He wrapped his arms firmly around her and said, "Sit down. I have a lot to tell you."

For a brief moment, she worried that maybe he'd decided she wasn't worth all this trouble and was calling the whole thing off, but then she chided herself for being silly and chalked it up to her frayed nerves. "What's going on?" she asked as she settled into the chair next to the one he'd been sitting in.

"Lots of things. First, I called Max—"

"Oh no!" She covered her eyes with her hand.

"I didn't mean to fight with him," Chris insisted.

"You *always* fight with him when you guys talk without a referee," she said with a groan.

He took her hand off her eyes so he could hold it and forced her to look at him. "Your safety needs to be addressed. Max told me I was being paranoid. He said we'd just change the date and location—again—and he would place lots of security at the gates. He hung up thinking that solved everything, but it doesn't solve anything."

"What do you mean?" Maybe he really was giving up altogether.

"I've been thinking about what your mom said about you and me going off and getting married somewhere, just the two of us. She said she'd never hold it against you because she wanted us to have our privacy."

"Okay . . ."

He released Tori's hand and turned the laptop to face her. "The arrangements will be finalized with one stroke of the Enter key."

Tori stared at the screen for several moments. He'd found a church in Athens where they could be married.

It took some effort to tear her gaze from the screen and meet his pleading eyes.

"I've done all the research. Made several phone calls—including to my own parents. Everyone agrees that we should do this."

"Even Max?" she asked.

Chris shook his head and waved his hand as if swatting away an irritating fly. "Max wants to own this day, and I get his point of view, I really do. But why can't we get married in Greece first—where no one knows but us? We can still do Max's wedding later—but think about it. This is our wedding. It's a day that should be filled with hope and joy and beginnings. We shouldn't have to worry about looking over our shoulders. We shouldn't be afraid on the one day that's supposed to be the happiest day of our lives. We need two witnesses, but no more than that. We should keep who we tell to only those witnesses. The fewer people who know, the better.

"We'll still be afraid on Max's wedding day, but if we do the real wedding first, we can spend Max's day focusing on our safety rather than trying to split our focus between the wedding and our safety."

It was a good plan. A secret wedding. He made a sound argument. Tori stared at him for several long moments as she considered everything before she said, "Our wedding . . . on our own terms."

She hit the Enter key.

Chapter 6

PAIGE
THE POST-GARTH ERA

WITH A SMILE, PAIGE CLICKED over to a Word document she'd put together earlier and printed out two copies of the packing list she'd created for the boys. Using the copies, the boys could mostly pack their own suitcases for the cruise for Athena's wedding. Ruby's phone call four weeks before had changed Paige's focus completely. She hadn't looked forward to anything this much in a long time—maybe not since the birth of her first child. The idea of going on a cruise felt like she was finally getting a new start, becoming the woman who had gone missing.

If she hadn't changed her life so completely over the last few months, she would never have agreed to let Ruby pay for her trip up front. But Ruby had agreed to let Paige pay her back in monthly installments, and now she was taking her boys to Greece! She could hardly fathom it.

She finished transcribing her last medical report of the day, then eyed her cell phone, willing it to buzz with an incoming text from Derryl. Over the last several months—basically since she'd broken both of their hearts by ending their romance—he'd turned into a dear friend and confidant. Well, except for the first few weeks after their breakup. Those were hard, especially spending Valentine's Day apart. Those days had been awkward and uncomfortable on every level. The two of them had worked in the same building, so they couldn't exactly avoid each other. They'd often crossed paths in the lobby, the elevator, and the café on the ground floor during lunch. She could only stand to eat in the back room of the dental office so many times to avoid the chance of running into Derryl on his way to or from work at the law firm one floor below.

Now Paige glanced at the clock as she closed the medical transcription program. Then she checked her e-mail one more time. Shawn would be walking in the door from school any minute. Derryl had sent her an e-mail, this one with a bunch of Jeff Foxworthy–type jokes beginning with "You

Know You're a Mormon If." She chuckled at each bullet. Derryl wouldn't understand half of the references, yet he knew she'd appreciate the jokes. He was such a sweet, sweet, *good* man.

Everything was easier now that she worked from home. No more running into Derryl at work. *More* contact with him in other ways—via e-mail and text. And it was thanks to him that she no longer worked in the same building and, even better, got to be home with her sons. Once a week she babysat Daisy's son, Sorrel, for a little extra money, and things were better now that she had a new divorce lawyer—referred to her by Derryl—who'd helped her renegotiate new child support and visitation arrangements.

The best of those changes was being able to work from home, and she had an awkward elevator ride to thank for that. A month after she'd officially broken up with Derryl, they'd ridden the same elevator—alone.

"Sorry you got stuck in here with me," she'd said.

"I'm not," Derryl countered with a wistful smile—from three feet away—respecting her decision and their new boundaries.

"Maybe we won't have these moments much longer. I'm hoping to find something else soon so I can be at home with my boys more."

They both knew Paige would give anything to be home with her boys as a stay-at-home mom again.

The doors opened, and Derryl got out. Paige thought nothing more about the brief encounter until the next day when Derryl texted, suggesting she train to be a medical transcriptionist and that he knew of a company looking to train new employees. She'd jumped at the chance, spending nights and whatever time she had previously spent with Derryl on the training. Now she worked from home, often at night when her two boys, ages four and seven, were asleep. She was there for them when they needed her. Best of all: no more day care. Plus, no more awkward run-ins with Derryl.

That first post-breakup text had broken the ice, and soon regular friendly texts and e-mails had begun.

Working from home, mastering her relationships, and now going on a cruise with her best friends . . . Paige felt like she should be pinching herself over it. She was really going on an exotic trip. The little girl from Utah who'd never been outside the States before. Sure, she'd visited her share of national parks, but the package that had arrived just yesterday contained the first passport she'd ever owned, plus two more for her boys, all of them rushed to get here in time for departure tomorrow.

The printer hummed, and when it was done, Paige snagged the packing lists. She'd used clip art to represent each item to pack, with a check box next to it, one for however many of each item was needed—one box for a swimsuit, but a whole row of boxes for socks, another row for shorts, and yet another for underwear.

She grabbed her phone and headed to the boys' room, where Nate sat on his bed coloring. She pulled a suitcase from under each bed. When Nate's suitcase, which was covered in Superman stickers, plopped beside him, he looked up questioningly at his mother. Suddenly he looked so much older to her, and she realized that in a way, she'd kept thinking of him as a three-year-old toddler. But he was four now, in preschool. The last year counted as a quarter of his life—and it had passed so quickly. In another year he'd start kindergarten. Nate had gained several inches and lost some of his baby fat. The sight was bittersweet.

"I made you a packing list," she said, setting it on his lap, interrupting him in the middle of drawing Superman flying over skyscrapers.

"Do we go in one more sleep?" he asked, holding up one blessedly still-chubby finger.

"Yep," she said. "Just one more. After you wake up in the morning, we'll eat breakfast and head to the airport."

"We'll fly high in the sky," he said, picking up where she left off, holding his arms out wide. "And the next day we'll get on a *huuuuge* ship and sail around the ocean to see lots of cool stuff."

"That's right." She ruffled his hair, feeling grateful that she'd been able to be around more in the last few months to watch him change and grow up—moments that would have been lost to her forever if she hadn't found a way out of her job at the office. Nate studied his packing list. He kept a bright red crayon in one hand, presumably for checking off boxes. He hopped off the bed and hurried to his dresser, apparently eager to follow the illustrated list.

Right then, Paige's phone went off with an incoming text. Her heart leapt a bit. Maybe it was Derryl. *He's not your boyfriend anymore*, she reminded herself. *No reason to get excited.* She'd have to put an end to the little thrills her body kept insisting on shooting through her in regard to Derryl. She'd ended their relationship for an important reason.

But the text wasn't from Derryl. She ordered herself not to be disappointed. After all, it was from one of her best friends, Daisy.

Got your voice mail saying you had a question about the trip. What can I help you with? You are still coming, aren't you?

She was most definitely still coming, thanks to the fact that Ruby's boyfriend had snagged a crazy good deal, so Paige's out-of-pocket expenses were minimal. If someone had told her a year ago that she'd be going on a cruise to celebrate a good friend's wedding, she would have laughed until she passed out. For starters, a year ago she didn't *have* any friends in California, good or otherwise, let alone any wiggle room in her budget. So much had changed for the better.

Paige walked out of the boys' room as Nate, looking studious and serious as he followed the list, dumped items into his suitcase, then marked off boxes. In the kitchen, she leaned against the window frame and looked out at the parking lot, where her car was visible—not Garth, the monstrosity she'd had when she arrived in California. Oh, no. He was laid to rest in junkyard heaven. Her former in-laws—who continued to be family to her despite their idiot jerk of a son—had bought themselves a brand-new Mercedes for their fortieth wedding anniversary—the first brand-new, custom-ordered, right-off-the-lot vehicle they'd ever owned. And they'd passed along their "old" Avalon to Paige. It had ten years and well over a hundred thousand miles on it, but compared to Garth, it was in fantastic shape and got far better gas mileage. Just one more area where she was saving money—no more gas-guzzling great beast, and no more emergency repairs.

She'd christened the Avalon "Shirley," after the red-haired heroine of *Anne of Green Gables*, who always kept a positive outlook and held to the belief that "tomorrow is fresh, with no mistakes in it." The name seemed like an appropriate way to celebrate the good changes and happiness that had come into her life after Garth. The old car and the time she'd driven it represented an immensely rough patch.

But now, between higher payments from Doug and no day-care expenses, Paige's little family was doing better financially than they had since moving to California almost a year earlier. That felt *good*. It was such a relief to be able to make a simple budget and keep to it, all without stressing out every day about how cheaply she could make dinner, how many meals she could stretch that whole chicken into, or how she'd afford birthday presents or gas.

Today was the first time she'd taken stock of all the good changes that had come into her life in the last year. As hard as the divorce and the move had been, today she felt a bit like a princess getting ready for a ball. Okay, except that she didn't have a prince. Yet. The time for that would come.

Maybe my next car will be named Camelot, she mused with a smile.

Back in January, she'd known deep down in the marrow of her bones that she was supposed to focus on her boys and on rebuilding *herself*. She hadn't ever taken the time to know who Paige was, to know what her personal strengths were. Doug was the first boy she'd ever dated, and after they'd married, he'd taken care of the finances—and pretty much everything else. After the divorce, she'd been left floundering, focusing on just getting through the next day and the next until her next paycheck. The last year had taught her that not only could she survive, but to heck with keeping her head above water; she could swim for shore and stand on firm ground again. She'd proven it to herself—and she'd done it all without a man.

After she'd ended things with Derryl, he'd given her suggestions and recommendations, sure, but she'd done all of the important legwork, from contacting the training company and working late hours to be qualified, to calling her new divorce attorney and laying out exactly what she wanted in a revised settlement—something she'd been too weak and confused about before. She hadn't known what to ask for then or how to ask for it. A few months before, all of it would have scared the daylights out of her.

Having a backbone—and using it—felt pretty good.

Another text came in, jolting Paige out of her reverie. Daisy again.

You ARE coming, right?

Paige smiled, realizing she hadn't replied. She typed out a response.

Of course! Wondered what time you were heading to the airport. I haven't flown out of LAX for a long time.

She clicked send and waited for a reply.

Give yourself a full hour and a half that time of day, and plan to be at the airport two hours early. It gets bogged down on a regular basis, and we don't want to miss this flight. We're going on a cruise!

Paige thanked Daisy and said she'd look for her in the morning. It would have been nice to drive down together, but Daisy's daughter, Stormy, and ex-husband—Stormy's dad—were coming with her. Paige pondered on the odd arrangement again. Jared was a great guy, something Paige had been witness to firsthand. Despite Daisy assuring her that they were just friends, would any man go along on a cruise "just because"—especially an ex? He *had* to be hoping for something more. Unless the two of them already had something more . . .

Or maybe I've been reading too many Regency romance novels.

Paige tucked the phone into her jeans pocket as the apartment door opened. Shawn ran in with a grin, his backpack rocking back and forth with each step. Paige opened her arms wide, loving the fact that she could greet him and hold him the moment he walked in from school. She pulled him onto her lap and kissed him on the temple.

"How was school? Learn anything interesting?"

He seemed to consider. "We started times tables." He stuck out his tongue, making a face.

"Oh, you'll do fine on those," Paige said. "You are such a hard worker. We'll get you some flashcards, and next thing you know, you'll have your times tables passed off through the twelves before anyone else in your class."

"Thanks, Mom." He leaned in and breathed in her perfume, something he did every day—a reason she made sure to put it on each morning. She hugged him back as her phone went off yet again. Shawn hopped off her lap, abandoned his backpack on the floor by her feet, and trotted over to the fridge to find an after-school snack. Nate ran out, having heard his big brother, and waved both packing lists high in the air.

"Look, Shawn! Look what Mom made. We get to pack our *own* suitcases."

Paige laughed, thinking that in ten years, when they were teenagers, they'd likely sing a different tune about "getting" to do their own work. She turned to her phone to check the text, wondering what Daisy was saying now.

But this time it was from Derryl. Her heart did a crazy dance in her chest.

You do have international service on your phone, don't you? Because I'll want to text you while you're gone. I'll miss you otherwise.

They rarely saw each other face-to-face anymore—they'd had two lunches since their breakup, one to introduce her to Derryl's friend who was doing the training for her job, and the other to introduce Paige to Derryl's divorce-lawyer friend. Paige had paid for her own meals, and in each case the lunch had had a business purpose, with a third party present. They were *not* dates. And it wasn't like he'd miss *seeing* her during the cruise. But she realized that she'd miss his texts and e-mails too if she had to go without them for nearly two weeks.

I think I'll have service, but I'll double-check tonight.

His reply came quickly.

If you don't, let me know. I'll pay for it just for the trip. You gotta be able to communicate with your friends, right?

He was right. Except for the fact that her closest friends would be with her on the trip.

All but Derryl. He counted as a friend, didn't he? She scoffed at herself. Of course he was a friend. And a dear, good man. The fact that he could maintain a platonic relationship after what they'd had—that said volumes. And she honestly didn't think he was keeping in touch on the off chance she'd change her mind or that things would someday change between them. She'd never given him that sliver of hope. Or herself, for that matter.

Yet she found herself praying that he'd never call their friendship quits. She needed it too much. Paige typed out a reply—one a bit more forward than she usually sent, but somehow it felt just right.

I definitely need international service. I'd miss you too much too.

Chapter 7

OLIVIA
THE DO-OVER DATE

"I THINK YOU SHOULD WEAR this." Marie held up the bright orange dress Livvy should have donated to a thrift store years ago.

Livvy scrunched her nose and tried to find something nice to say about why she'd rather not go out to dinner with her husband looking like the great pumpkin. When she'd been thin, the dress had looked cute. Now that she wasn't exactly thin anymore, the dress was, well . . . not so cute.

Mandy saved her by yanking the monstrosity from her sister's hands and saying, "That's fun, Marie, but she doesn't want to look *fun*; she wants to look classy. Let's find classy clothes."

Marie went back to the walk-in closet from which she'd unearthed the orange dress. Mandy widened her eyes at Livvy. "Why would you even own such a thing? Hurry and throw it away before Marie comes back. It embarrasses me to be your daughter when I know stuff like that is lurking in your closet."

"What's lurking?" Tyler asked. He'd come in to join the girls as Livvy readied herself for her date with Nick. They were going to have a night out. The *whole* night. Just the two of them.

"Scary things," Mandy said. "Mom just proved that monsters in closets really do exist."

Marie practically exploded from the closet. "There's monsters in here?"

Tyler snickered, apparently glad to have found that joining the girls didn't mean he had to do girl things. He took the opportunity to torment his little sister by pulling his shirt over his head, putting up his arms, stretching his fingers out like claws, and making growling noises that sounded more like he was clearing his throat than the monster he pretended to be.

Marie shoved him before Livvy could get between them.

Mandy rolled her eyes and moved past them all so she could take a turn browsing through the closet. She came out holding a dress bag from Neiman Marcus. She grinned. "You should wear this."

Livvy blinked at the bag she didn't recognize and knew for a fact didn't belong in her closet. "What is that? I've never seen it before." Livvy took the bag from her daughter's hands and squinted at the semiopaque vinyl in an attempt to see inside. Where had it come from?

"Try it on. I bet it's perfect." Mandy smacked Tyler's hands down so he'd stop teasing Marie and herded the kids out of the room. "I'll be back in a few minutes to see."

Livvy caught the gleam in her daughter's eye as she shut the door. "That girl knows something," Livvy said to herself.

She unzipped the bag to reveal a note pinned to the dress. Nick's handwriting. Too excited to read the note, she worked faster to free the dress from the packaging.

"Nicolas Robbins, what have you done?"

She gasped when she saw the black, floor-length gown. Mandy had said she needed something classy, but this dress was so much more than classy.

It was *sexy*, beautiful—perfect.

She carefully unpinned the note:

My dearest Liv,

I know we agreed to the verbal communication thing, but I figured you'd forgive me hiding behind a note on this one. I want you to know how beautiful you are, so I bought a dress to match the woman. Wear it tonight for me. I can't wait to see you in it. I love you. Don't fuss too much with your hair. I plan on messing it up anyway.

Love,

Me (You'd better know who me is)

She smiled. The tips of her ears burned as an outward manifestation of all she felt toward Nicolas Robbins. They were here in a new place of talking—of being honest and open with each other, a place she'd forgotten existed. It felt so wonderful that sometimes it also felt unbelievable. Sure, things weren't perfect all the time, but Livvy had come to wonder if the imperfections were the things that told you your heart was still beating.

She slid into the dress, reaching behind her to pull up the zipper, and turned to the freestanding mirror by her dresser. In shock, Livvy covered her mouth with one hand. The full-length gown made her feel tall and elegant. The black color and cut of the dress made her look curvy instead of motherly. Had Nick somehow bewitched the mirror so it would show her how he saw her? Because she never remembered looking like this.

"You're beautiful," Mandy said from behind her. Livvy hadn't heard the door open.

She couldn't stop the smile spreading across her face as she met her daughter's gaze in the mirror. "Why did he do this?" she asked, knowing Mandy had some insider information.

Mandy lifted a shoulder. "He said it was long overdue."

Marie bounced into the room and jumped on the bed. "That's not what he said. He said it was a *do-over*."

Mandy cut a glare at her sister. "He just said you guys were overdue for a night away together. Right, Marie?" Mandy used her don't-argue-with-me tone.

Marie seemed to be abashed and hurried to nod.

Livvy crossed her arms over her chest, loving the way the dress swished around her legs as she shifted. "What is all this about?" she asked, facing Marie.

"Marie! Mandy!" Tyler called from the hallway. "I need your help!"

Marie looked torn between spilling her guts to her mom and seeing what her brother needed.

"Now!"

"Sounds like he really needs us," Mandy said, pulling her sister off the bed and out of the room. "We'll let you finish getting ready. Bye, Mom."

The door shut again.

That wasn't suspicious *at all*. Livvy smirked and considered going out to force a confession, but it seemed she'd ruin a surprise if she did. If Nick wanted to give her a surprise, then she wouldn't do anything to ruin it.

Instead, she shook her head and finished dressing, rethinking her jewelry choices so she could match the perfection of her new dress. She needed a necklace that would skim across her collarbone rather than the longer chain she'd planned on. She could still wear the strappy black heels she'd set out because they matched, thankfully. And in spite of Nick's instruction to do otherwise, she spent *a lot* of time on her hair. She wanted to make sure it looked nice enough to merit being messed up.

By the time she wandered downstairs, Nick stood by the door in a jet-black suit, waiting for her.

With flowers.

Livvy didn't remember the last time flowers had been involved in their relationship. She descended the stairs, feeling curious about the formality of this evening. Their gazes were locked as she crossed the floor to him, and she smiled as she accepted the flowers. "Wow. They're beautiful."

He gave her an appreciative smile of his own. "I was going to say the same thing about you. Absolutely beautiful."

She blushed, not being able to help it, feeling like she was a teen going on a first date. She'd married a seriously handsome man, and what woman wouldn't blush when a handsome man showered compliments on her?

"I'll go put these in water." Livvy started to turn toward the kitchen, but Nick stopped her.

"Leave them here. I'll text Mandy to do it. We don't want to be late." He held out his arm, and she took it. Joy filled her all the way to her toes. In the morning, the book-club ladies were boarding an airplane bound for Rome. She was the only one who wouldn't be there. She'd worried that maybe depression would settle in somewhere over missing the trip and the wedding, but in that moment, she found she honestly didn't envy them anything.

There wasn't anywhere in the world she wanted to be more than at her husband's side.

Nick settled her into the passenger side of the car before going around and letting himself in. Once they were driving, she caught him neglecting to watch the road several times so he could look at her.

She didn't bother to tell him to keep his eyes on the road. If they got into an accident while he looked at her with that heat in his eyes? Well . . . there were worse ways to die.

A smile of contentment found its way to her lips when he pulled out in front of Liaison, Livvy's favorite French restaurant. They hadn't been to Liaison in years.

He opened her car door for her, kissed her hand, and led her inside.

Once they were seated and had their orders taken, she laced her fingers on the table in front of her. "So what is all this for?" she asked. "If we weren't already married, I'd think you were trying to propose."

Nick grinned, the wrinkles at the corners of his hazel eyes deepening in that way she loved. "Do I need a reason to treat my wife to a nice evening?"

No. He didn't need a reason. But that didn't mean there wasn't a reason. She let it go. If he wanted to be mysterious and amazing, she'd just go with it.

She allowed herself to stop wondering and guessing and relaxed into the fact that she was having a great night.

They ate and walked down memory lane, laughing about things she hadn't thought about in years, getting more serious when the subjects of their conversation required contemplation, and laughing some more because Nick really was a funny guy.

When they left the restaurant, they didn't go home. She swallowed hard as he pulled up to the entrance of the Renaissance hotel.

The Renaissance was uncomfortably close to the airport. It sent a shiver of sadness over her, and though she wouldn't trade places with any of her friends, she felt the sting of being so close to where they would be leaving from in the morning. She took a deep breath, determined to focus on being with Nick, not on what she'd be missing.

He checked them in and led the way to their room. She was hyper-aware of the way his hand stayed at the small of her back. She loved that he'd returned to the old way of always needing to touch her when they were together. It made her feel connected and secure.

He opened the door, waited for her to enter, and wrapped his arms around her as the door fell closed again. "You thought I was kidding when I promised to mess up your hair, didn't you?"

"I felt pretty sure you meant it," she said before letting him kiss her.

They stood there, getting more lost and tangled up in each other by the second, before he finally pulled away and put an arm out to keep her from reclosing the distance.

"I have something for you."

"How could you possibly have anything more? This whole night has been perfect."

He grinned. "And you know what a perfectionist I am. To top *perfect* will be my best achievement." He took her hand and sat her on the bed. Then he took out the remote to the TV and pressed On.

"You brought me to a hotel to watch TV?" she asked with a smirk.

"Wait for it," he said.

The big screen filled with an image of an old book with the words "Once Upon a Time" embossed in the leather. The camera panned out to reveal the book being held by someone. It pulled out more to reveal that the someone was their daughter Mandy.

The screen suddenly had her full attention.

Mandy gave the camera a coy glance before she returned her focus to the pages of the book and began to read. "Once upon a time there was a daddy."

The TV picture split into a second pane revealing Livvy's stepdaughter, Jessica. "Some of us call him Dad," Jessica said.

The picture split into thirds, and her stepson, Kohl, appeared. "Some of us call him Grumpy."

"You mean Grandpa," Jessica corrected.

"Whatever." Kohl shrugged.

The picture split again, only this time it revealed all six of their kids in their own window panes. Mandy resumed reading. "One day Dad met a charming, beautiful woman who made him and his two kids happy."

"Some of us call her Livvy," Kohl said.

"Some of us call her Mom," Tyler said.

Marie giggled in her own little frame and covered her mouth with her hands. Livvy laughed along with her youngest.

"But we all call her Wonderful," Chad said.

Livvy blinked hard to keep the blur of tears from impeding her view of the screen.

The background for Chad revealed his dorm room at school, whereas Kohl's background looked like the inside of a tent. How had they pulled off this video when the family was stretched all across the world?

Mandy turned the page in her book. "Once Dad—"

"Also called Grumpy," Tyler interrupted.

"Dad!" The rest of the kids in their frames shouted at Tyler.

Mandy snorted but kept reading. "—had met this woman, Livvy, he knew he'd do everything in his power to make her happy for her whole entire life."

"Except sometimes," Chad said, putting up a finger.

Jessica nodded. "Sometimes he didn't make her happy."

Tyler widened his eyes and made a ridiculous face. "Sometimes he made her crazy."

Chad sighed and shook his head. "And sometimes he failed epically at making an anniversary special."

"And sometimes he needed to say sorry." Kohl said, making Livvy's heart ping at all the implications of what *sorry* meant to Kohl.

She wiped at her cheeks and sniffed to keep her nose from dripping on her dress. She took Nick's hand and squeezed hard.

Mandy turned the page again. "But he was a good dad. He always taught his kids that when they did something wrong . . ."

"They had the opportunity to make it right with a *do-over*," Chad finished.

Kohl put on reading glasses that made him look like a professor and pretended to look something up in a dictionary that looked suspiciously like an ammunitions reference guide. "A *do-over* is when we get a clean slate and we try again."

"Epic fails require epic do-overs," Chad said.

Tyler snickered. "Dad needs something epic, then."

Mandy cut a glare toward Tyler's window. "So Dad—"

"Grumpy," Chad said.

"Dad!" Mandy corrected.

Marie giggled.

Mandy rolled her eyes. "Took Mom—"

"Livvy," Kohl said.

"Wonderful," Jessica added.

"On a special date," Mandy finished.

"There was a pretty dress," Jessica said.

Chad pretended to play a violin. "There was music."

The restaurant *had* played classical music in the background, which Livvy figured had to be close enough.

Tyler suddenly had a fork in his hand and was pretending to eat. "There was dinner; that's my favorite."

Livvy laughed at his antics.

"Best of all, there was both of them," Mandy said with a satisfied sigh before she looked up with a startled expression. "But what's this?"

"There's more?" Kohl asked.

"There is more!" Jessica clapped her hands. "It involves water."

Tyler pinched a rubber duck to make it squeak. "Is it a bath?"

Livvy cast a sideways glance at Nick, wondering if there was a bubble bath in their evening plans and, if so, hoping Nick hadn't apprised the kids of that kind of embarrassing information.

Marie giggled some more, which made both Nick and Livvy laugh as they watched. Nick wiped at the shine in his eyes. Livvy didn't bother wiping away any more tears since she was a sodden mess from all her crying.

Mandy shook her head. "No, it's more water than that."

Livvy raised her eyebrows at Nick in question, but he just grinned and shook his head. Had he gone out and bought a hot tub?

Chad held up one of those obscenely small Speedos. "Is it a swimming pool?"

"No. Even more water than that," Mandy answered.

Definitely not a hot tub, then.

Kohl looked at a map behind him and pointed to the space that separated the continents between them. "Is it an ocean?"

"Now we're talking!" Jessica said.

Mandy held up her hand to the other frames on the screen. "If you'd all stop interrupting me, I could read to the end!" She cleared her throat and flipped through a few pages. "Ah, yes. Here we are. So Grumpy—"

"Don't you mean Dad?" Chad asked.

Marie covered her eyes and shook her head as she laughed harder than ever.

"Right," Mandy said. "Dad. So Dad booked a cruise, a new cruise, because he knows Mom—"

"Wonderful Livvy," Kohl and Jessica said together.

"Wants to see her friend get married in Greece."

Livvy choked on a sob and covered her mouth. How had he known?

"Greece?" all the other kids asked from their various panes, all turning to where Mandy's pane sat on the screen.

"Greece!" Mandy said, turning the page of her book again for effect. "Because Dad—"

"I'm not calling Daddy Grumpy," Marie said, looking horrified from her pane.

"Didn't want Livvy to miss out on the opportunity to be with her friends. So he planned it all with the help of their awesome kids."

"That's us!" they all shouted.

"He took her to dinner. And to a hotel, where they would wait for morning to come and for the plane that would take them away to Rome. Mom doesn't have to worry about anything because her bags are already packed. And because Jessica"—Jessica waved—"is staying in Newport with the kids. And Chad promises to study. And Kohl promises to stay out of danger. So . . ."

"Happy do-over anniversary!" they all yelled before the screen went dark.

Livvy mopped at her cheeks and wished he'd warned her not to do her makeup because he'd obviously planned on messing that up too.

"Tell me those are happy tears," Nick said as he tightened his grip on her hand.

She threw her arms around his neck and laughed through the tears. "They're so much more than that. I can't believe you've done all this. How did you get the kids to come together to do all that?"

"Chad's taking a filmmaking class in school, so it doubled as a class assignment. He arranged everything and set it all up. And just so you know, Marie is getting a raise in her allowance for being the only one of the kids not willing to call me Grumpy."

Livvy laughed some more, feeling so much love for her family and husband that there was barely room in her to draw breath. "How did you know about Athena's wedding?"

He turned to face her. "Mandy told me about it the night you got the phone call. I knew it was important to you, but I also understood why you didn't say anything. I called Ruby as soon as I knew. I think I woke her up."

He took a deep breath. "I really am sorry about our anniversary last year, Liv. And hope you'll accept this do-over as a replacement."

"Stop talking, Mr. Robbins. You're forgiven. I only want you to kiss me."

So he did.

That man *really* knew how to kiss her.

Chapter 8
DAISY
STOWAWAY

"ARE YOU SURE YOU HAVE the cruise documents?"

Daisy glared at Jared's smirk, and despite having checked half a dozen times since they'd gotten to the pier in Rome—*Rome!*—she pulled her purse in front of her and unzipped the pocket where she kept all the documentation, passports, and confirmations. Jared—Daisy's ex-husband—found her neurotic fear of losing them hilarious, even though she'd seen them forty minutes ago. She'd always been this way, even when they were married, which was how Jared knew this traveling quirk. She couldn't *not* check, and he knew it.

"I'm going to throw you off this boat," she said as she verified that she had everyone's passports plus all the information they needed to check onto the ship—which was why they were in line in the first place.

Jared raised his eyebrows. "I'd love to see you try." The silkiness in his voice made her neck heat up. Was the comment a kind of invitation to . . . what? She refused to let her thoughts go *there*, but his words provided one more layer of confusion to an increasingly large pile that had been building up over the last few months—ever since she'd moved to an apartment half a block from where he lived with their daughter, Stormy, who had just turned eighteen. Ever since Daisy had given birth to another man's baby—her *other* ex-husband's. Ever since Jared had somehow become important in her life again. But it wasn't a *romantic* relationship that had grown between them, which was why the seductive quality of his comment confused her. Their current relationship was as unromantic as it could be. He'd looked up home remedies for breast engorgement when he'd come over and found her crying from the pain she couldn't remember how to alleviate. He'd sometimes pick up a case of diapers from Costco when he went there for protein shakes and cheese. When Daisy had gotten sick last month, he'd slept on the couch to help take care of Sorrel so she could get a full night's sleep and so that Stormy wouldn't be late for her new job that started the next day.

Definitely not romantic. Never mind the fact that they'd also been divorced for nearly fifteen years, or the whole other-man's-child issue, or the fact that Daisy had been divorced from her *second* husband, Paul, for just over two months, though it felt much longer.

Stormy returned from buying a cannoli. She'd refused the food on the plane and was "starving her face off," so Daisy had given her five dollars and wished her luck on finding a food vendor that would take American bills. Apparently she'd been successful. She took a bite while looking at Daisy a little too closely. After swallowing, she wiped the corners of her mouth with her napkin. "Are you blushing because you guys are flirting again?"

Now it was time for Jared to blush too, though Daisy easily joined him for a second round. They both looked away—Daisy checking the documents again, and Jared squatting down and peeking at Sorrel, who was blessedly asleep after crying for the last hour on the plane. If Daisy could have bought every person on that plane a pony to make up for the misery of her baby's tears, she would have. Instead, she'd pretended not to see their glares and prayed he would stop crying—which he did just ten minutes before arrival. Now it seemed he'd worn himself out. Daisy's eyes moved from the documents to Jared, who was rocking the car seat slightly with one hand and tucking the blanket under Sorrel's chin with the other. The sight stopped her heart and added yet *another* layer to that pile of confusion. When she looked at Stormy's questioning expression, Daisy turned away and worked on reorganizing her purse while the line moved forward at a snail's pace.

Stormy took a step closer to her and lowered her voice slightly, as if mindful of being overheard even though she was blatantly ignoring Daisy's avoidance of the subject. "So, you still think Dad coming on the cruise with us is *no big deal?*" She said the last three words in a lower voice Daisy assumed was supposed to be an imitation of how Daisy had explained it to her nearly a month ago.

Daisy was quick to explain, again, the real reason for the odd arrangement. "We'd already been talking about a graduation trip for you when Ruby called me about Athena's wedding, so this was a way to kill two birds with one stone." Daisy shrugged to further emphasize how casual a decision it was to have all of them take the cruise, but she couldn't help adding more details. "And Gabriel worked out such a great deal, and I wouldn't have been able to come with Sorrel by myself, and I couldn't leave him, and—"

"Blah, blah, blah, blah, blah," Stormy cut in, making a talking motion with her free hand. "Admit it—you're hot for Dad."

"Stormy!" Daisy hissed, grabbing Stormy's "talking" hand and giving her a sharp look. "Stop it. I'm not kidding about this. Stop."

Stormy seemed startled at the gravity in Daisy's voice. She'd been teasing Daisy about this for weeks, and Daisy had been shutting down the jokes for just as long. But in the last few days—as she'd finalized plans with Jared, set about packing, and *really* thought about the trip, her own questions had melted together with Stormy's and some of the comments a few of the book-group ladies had made, including implications regarding Jared's coming along. Tori had flat out asked at the last book group if Daisy and Jared were "a thing," which Daisy had refuted, of course. Had something changed in the weeks since that comment? Or was Daisy simply the last one to see things the way everyone else already seemed to?

"Enough," Daisy added for good measure, raising her eyebrows and not blinking. "Okay?"

"Okay. Don't have a coronary."

Daisy shot her another look, and Stormy dipped her head in as much of an apology as Daisy could have hoped for. "Sorry."

"Sorry for what?" Jared asked from behind, then tilted his head forward when they both looked at him. "Holding up the line?"

A five-foot gap had widened between them and the rest of the line. They picked up their bags—Jared picked up Sorrel's carrier with his free hand—and moved forward. A few minutes later they were at the check-in desk, and Daisy handed over her documents.

"Mr. and Mrs. Herriford," the clerk asked in a thick accent. Daisy couldn't even pretend to guess where the clerk was from.

"No, Mr. Jared Herriford and Mrs. Daisy Atkins."

The clerk looked between them, and Daisy shifted her weight. "Daisy Atkins and Sorrel Atkins are sharing one room." She tapped the document that had the correct names, then pointed a thumb over her shoulder at Jared. "He's sharing with Stormy Herriford."

The clerk looked between her and Jared, then nodded and moved on to the next document without asking more questions. He read each

name out loud, then compared them to the photos on their passports.
Sorrel didn't need a passport, just his birth certificate.

"Sorrel Atkins?"

Jared lifted the baby carrier, and the clerk smiled and checked something
off on the paperwork.

"Stormy Herriford."

"Here," Stormy said as if she were at school and the teacher was calling
role. Everyone laughed, and some of the tension skittered away.

"You have cabins in the same hall but not right next to each other.
Will that be all right?"

"It's fine," Jared and Daisy said at the same time.

The clerk double-checked the documents and passports, stamped
them, typed something into his computer, then handed them their ID
cards, which would be used as a charge card on board as well as identi-
fication to get on and off the ship. The clerk took their bags much like
the airline attendants had sixteen hours earlier and assured them their
luggage would be in their cabins by six o'clock. Daisy kept her purse and
the diaper bag. They were ushered to another line where the awkwardness
dissipated as they reviewed the different port stops and the things they
wanted to see.

They were going to Greece. Holy cow! And now that Stormy was going
to back off of her inappropriate comments, everything would be okay.

A woman farther up in line turned and waved at Daisy. It was
Shannon. Daisy had spoken to her on the plane for a bit but hadn't had a
chance to say much since her hands were full with a baby and a teenager.
Daisy waved back and smiled, thinking how great it was that everyone in
the book club had been able to make the trip.

"Are you sure you have the ID cards?" Jared asked Daisy after a few
minutes. "You didn't leave them on the counter, did you?"

"Stop it!" Daisy said, but she dug through her purse to check all the
same.

"Okay, okay," said a voice Daisy didn't recognize. She looked up from
her purse hunting to see a dark-skinned young man in black pants and a
green shirt with the cruise line's logo waving Stormy and Jared to a photo
backdrop of the ship. A stand to the left of the photo had a lifesaver with
the word *Welcome* printed on it. "Come on, come on," he said to Daisy,
who was lagging behind.

"What's this?" Daisy asked. She tucked a lock of hair behind her ear
and started moving toward them.

"A welcome photo. Duh," Stormy said. Jared began to unstrap Sorrel from his car seat.

"Don't wake him up," Daisy said, putting the diaper bag down.

"The stowaway has to be in the photo," Jared explained as he gently lifted little Sorrel out of his car seat. Through some weird deal Gabriel had been able to work out, kids under twelve were free on the cruise, without which Sorrel would have been the same price as an adult. Because of the deal, Stormy had started calling her baby brother a stowaway every time they talked about the cruise, and the nickname had stuck. Sorrel was almost four months old, and, despite a difficult pregnancy, he was healthy and strong and doing great. Daisy had been able to adjust her work schedule so she worked from home thirty hours a week and only went to the office for one day—during which time her friend Paige watched Sorrel. Daisy couldn't help but admire Jared's quiet confidence as he cooed at her son. He shifted the tiny body into a football-type hold while the photographer kept ushering them to "Get together. Get together."

They automatically stood with Jared on one side of Stormy and Daisy on the other. "No, no," the photographer said, moving forward and pulling Stormy out from between her parents. "Sweethearts together. Sweethearts together." It sounded more like *sweat-hots toogeder*.

"We're not sweethearts," Daisy said, refusing to move as Stormy obediently complied with the directions and moved to Jared's other side.

"Sweethearts together. Sweethearts together."

"But we're not—"

"Take the stowaway," Jared said.

Daisy looked up at him and complied, taking Sorrel in her arms and shifting him so he curved into her. It was surreal that he was in her life, surreal and yet such a blessing. She was determined to be the kind of mother she hadn't been to her daughters. Despite that commitment, however, she was aggravated by the fact that he'd been woken up from his nap and that this photographer seemed determined to make Jared and Daisy out to be the couple when they weren't.

"We're not a couple," she said as Jared put his arm around her shoulders and stepped so close she could smell his cologne—a fragrance she didn't recognize but suddenly wanted to spray on her pillow. The feel of his arm across her shoulders and the way his fingers brushed her upper arm made her shiver slightly. She hoped he couldn't tell.

"Smile, smile," the photographer said.

"But—"

"Just smile," Jared and Stormy said at the same time through cheesy grins.

Daisy looked up to see the photographer stepping behind his camera. Knowing she was going to be forever frozen with an idiotic expression on her face if she didn't comply, she straightened her shoulders, tossed her hair back, and gave her best smile.

Snap.

"Okay, okay. Move on, move on."

Jared took a still-sleepy Sorrel from her arms and put him back in the carrier while Daisy shouldered her diaper bag and marinated in more confusing thoughts all over again. She'd worked so hard to push away people's teasing about Jared coming on the cruise with her that she hadn't really looked at how the arrangement, well, *looked*. Why hadn't she considered how awkward it would be when they appeared so much like a real family?

She glanced at Jared, who was making baby sounds at Sorrel, then Stormy, who watched her with a raised eyebrow, and then she looked at Jared again. She couldn't help it.

There had been a time when she was absolutely in love with that man. He'd filled her heart and life in every way. They'd had a child together, and he'd gladly stepped into the role as father to Daisy's oldest daughter, December, from a previous relationship—he'd been so good to all of them. They'd been happy. But then . . . Her brain wouldn't go there. It wouldn't explore the *but then*. It had been years since she'd found herself stuck in the muddy memories of that time, and she realized with a shock that she felt no need to go back to them. Life changed people, and despite the past heartbreak he'd caused her, she couldn't deny that Jared was a better man now than he'd been when their marriage had fallen apart. She was a better woman too. The experiences they'd gone through apart from each other had made them better.

For each other?

Her cheeks heated up again. Was she really thinking about Jared and her as a couple again? As "a thing"? The thought embarrassed her. What would Jared make of such ideas?

"Come on, Mama," Jared said, bringing her back to the present.

Daisy looked up at him. He winked, lightly swinging the carrier back and forth. She met his eyes—eyes she'd once become lost in—and felt the tingly thrill she hadn't felt for a really long time. His smile changed from one of teasing to one of . . . she didn't really know how to interpret it. Understanding? Pleasure?

It could never work. You both have way too much baggage to even consider another relationship.

It didn't work the first time; why would it work a second time?

He doesn't think of you like that.

How could you ever really trust him again?

And yet . . . he didn't look away. He held her eyes and seemed to feel as vulnerable as she did.

He's been amazing with Sorrel.

He's helped you with things he had no reason to help you with.

You know each other.

You have a daughter together.

"Mother," Stormy said in a formal tone that broke Daisy out of her trance. She looked at her daughter, whose expression was completely blank. When Stormy spoke again, her formal tone bordered on a British accent. "Shall we make way to the buffet, do you think?"

Daisy was confused by the formality until she realized that Stormy was purposely not teasing her about the way she'd been gazing into Jared's eyes just now.

Jared cleared his throat and walked ahead of them, allowing Daisy to take in his wide shoulders, narrow hips, the way the muscles in his forearms bulged beneath his skin just enough to remind her that he'd been working out regularly the last year. He hadn't been dating anyone. And he'd been so attentive to her, not just after Sorrel was born but beforehand too. He turned to look over his shoulder. "The stowaway and I are totally going to beat you guys."

Stowaway. It was a pretty good description of the thoughts and feelings Daisy hadn't accounted for in her packing list. She was crazy to be thinking these thoughts. Absolutely insane. Yet one question stood out above all others. Why *had* Jared come on this cruise? He'd taken work off, paid for his own ticket, and volunteered to come when she'd told him she didn't think she'd be able to make it work with Sorrel by herself—she hadn't asked him to. So why?

He glanced over his shoulder again as though making sure Stormy and Daisy were following, and in the process caught Daisy's eye once more. The look lasted only a moment, but she knew, she *knew*, that he'd come on this cruise to be with her.

That stowaway thought sent another shiver through her entire body as her perception took a dramatic shift and she asked herself what she was going to do about it.

Chapter 9

ILANA
REALITY CHECK

FOR THE THIRD TIME SINCE leaving her cabin and her napping husband, Ilana pulled out the brochure with the map of the ship to be sure she was headed in the right direction. She paused at the railing surrounding deck ten and looked out, breathing in the salty air and enjoying the breeze whipping her curly hair around her face. The ship had left port an hour ago, and the Italian coastline ran alongside at a distance as ocean water churned from the giant propeller at the back of the ship. A wide, frothy wake went out from the ship in a V shape, but beyond, the sea was a huge, sparkling sheet of blue, blue water. Ilana had never been on a cruise before, despite being married to a doctor. Any extra money after medical school loan payments had gone toward fertility treatments.

That was no longer an option, of course. At the thought, Ilana's hand instinctively went to her bag to assure herself that the manila envelope was still inside. The reminder was enough to break her from the mesmerizing view and remind her why she'd consulted the map in the first place—the book-club ladies were meeting at the Blue Moon Café to discuss the details of Athena's wedding. Ilana reached the restaurant doors five minutes early and peered inside. She double-checked the sign above the doors to confirm that this was the place she'd circled on the brochure. As expected, it was technically closed, as Athena had said it would be, but the door wasn't locked; their small group had reserved the space during off hours.

Ilana had hoped for a few minutes of privacy to review the paperwork again. She'd tell Ethan about it soon. Somehow. Her breathing turned shallow, and her stomach twisted with nerves at the thought of the papers inside the envelope.

I could really use a Vicodin about now. Ten milligrams—or maybe just five—and the edge would be taken off her emotions. But no. As good as that would feel—and she suspected it would have a stronger effect now that she'd been off all meds for a while—she didn't do that anymore. She shook off the thought and pushed the door open. As she stepped onto the carpeted floor, she reached into her jeans pocket to touch the ninety-day chip recently presented to her at the outpatient NA meeting she'd attended after graduating from the in-patient program. The coin-like chip was a tangible reminder of the journey she'd taken into sobriety. She clasped it tightly in one hand, determined to get her four-month chip, which she'd either earn or forfeit during the cruise.

I can't lose my chip; I've worked too hard for it. Emotions suck, but I have to deal with them.

She'd deal with the different what-ifs surrounding the paperwork, but first she had to get over the urge to self-medicate. *I'm powerless, not helpless*, she thought, repeating the mantra she'd memorized. Other reminders she'd learned through therapy and rehab followed. *Sobriety is a journey, not an event. Fear is the thief of dreams.* She swallowed, glad her purse didn't have any Vicodin—not anymore, anyway. But she *was* on a cruise ship and would likely run into alcohol everywhere. Even a wine cooler could be enough to send her into a tailspin, and she'd be back to working toward a white chip, which represented one measly day of sobriety.

Ilana took a seat near a window, where she closed her eyes and breathed deeply to ward off the adrenaline and anxiety mounting inside her. Twenty deep breaths later she opened her eyes and looked around. She was still alone except for a worker who'd come out with a sweeper to clean dust and crumbs from the carpet. Ilana smiled at the young man, then checked her watch and looked at the door again. None of the ladies were here yet, and she couldn't help herself any longer; she had to look at the papers again. She shoved the chip back into her pocket before opening her bag and pulling out the manila envelope that could change everything.

Her hands still trembled when she opened the envelope and slid out the international adoption forms, which were almost complete now. Her heart hammered against her rib cage, but this time it wasn't the often-unpleasant sensation of needing relief from her emotions; this was anticipation mixed with excitement.

Soon. She'd tell Ethan soon that she'd accepted the idea of adoption— finally. He'd wanted it for years, but she'd stubbornly clung to the idea of bearing a child herself, until that chance was lost to her with a hysterectomy back in January.

Had that really been less than a year ago? Her entire life had been turned on its head since then. The only constant she had was Ethan. He'd been so patient as she'd dealt with her surgeries—two of them—plus her addiction to the pills that had taken the grief away, at least momentarily. Through it all, she knew he still hoped she'd agree to adopt, but he wisely hadn't broached the topic. Only last month she'd decided to look into it on her own, not wanting to get his hopes up, and she'd determined that going international would likely be easier. A birth mom in the States, with her choice of adoptive mothers, was far less likely to place her baby with someone recently out of rehab.

But I'm clean, and I'll stay clean. Please don't keep me from having a baby because of a stupid set of choices.

Who she was pleading with she didn't want to think about, not too much—she'd come to accept the idea of not *hating* God, exactly, but still, they weren't on the greatest of terms either. At this point, she'd come to accept two ideas about God: He existed, and He wasn't necessarily malevolent. That was about as far as she could take religion at this point.

The women who had come into her life over the last year—the mishmash of personalities and ages and backgrounds from the book club she'd joined on a whim—had led her to improve her life and overcome a lot. So maybe, just maybe, they were a blessing from God.

And maybe He'd see fit to give her a child. Make her a mother. Ilana no longer wondered if her baby would have her curly hair or Ethan's green eyes. Instead, she wondered if her child would be Chinese or African or another nationality she hadn't yet considered.

A blank line for Ethan's signature stared at her, the white spot jumping off the page, obvious and glaring. Ethan would be thrilled . . . right?

The door opened, and Ilana heard voices. She shoved the papers back into the envelope, nearly bending a corner of one in the process. By the time the papers were tucked safely into her bag and she looked up, Paige and Daisy were halfway across the floor.

"Ilana!" Paige said. She was holding her two boys' hands but released them to rush over and give Ilana a big hug. "It's so good to see you!"

Ilana's arms went forward but didn't quite wrap around Paige at first; Ilana had never been a touchy-feely person, and she was still getting used to hugs from people like Paige and Ruby. Ilana relaxed her arms and managed to hug Paige back. "It's good to see you too."

Paige's boys had climbed onto chairs. One dumped out the sugar packets from their container and was arranging them in stacks by color. The other was shaking salt and pepper into little mounds. Ilana wasn't sure whether to be horrified or impressed; the boys weren't loud or obnoxious, but they *were* making a mess. What would she do as their mother? She'd judged many a mother in the grocery store with whiny, tantrum-throwing toddlers, priding herself with the thought that *her* kids would never be loud or disruptive in public. But would they?

Before she could analyze her future mothering any further, Daisy had thrown her arm around Ilana's shoulders in a side hug. Daisy held her little boy—now what, four or five months old?—on her other hip. She bounced him slightly as he gnawed on his chubby fist, sending drool dripping off his chin.

Ilana had already pondered diapers and throw-up and late-night feedings. *But I forgot about the drool.* She shuddered. Drool grossed her out. She'd rather change a hundred diapers than have baby drool all over her. And then the universe decided to mock her by not giving her drool *or* diapers.

Daisy tugged a spit cloth of some kind from her diaper bag and, one-handed, wiped the baby's face, shirt, and hands. The little boy's face scrunched up suddenly, and he began to wail—long and loud.

"What's wrong?" Ilana asked, in awe at Daisy's ability to not panic in the face of tears and screams. "Is he okay?"

Daisy checked her watch as if the time had something to do with her son's sudden switch in temper. "He's hungry. I forgot to make up a bottle before I left the cabin. Would you hold him while I do that? It'll only take a second."

Before Ilana could answer, her arms were filled with fifteen pounds of screaming baby. Ilana tried to bridle the anxiety threatening to work its way up her throat. Daisy seemed perfectly at ease as she found a plastic container with premeasured portions of formula and calmly clicked open the lid to one section. She tapped the powder into a bottle, then measured the water. The process seemed to go on and on. Ilana strained to watch every step, hoping to memorize it, all the while trying to mimic the way Daisy had bounced the kid on her hip, to no avail. His cries grew louder, his face redder, and soon he was desperately reaching for his mother, practically throwing himself in Daisy's direction. Ilana clung to him and tried to right his body from the near backbend he'd managed. The louder he cried, the harder her heart pounded and her stomach twisted.

Come on. Calm down. Please.

"Here," Paige said, reaching out. "Let me try."

Ilana felt a bit guilty for how eagerly she handed him over. He didn't stop crying completely in Paige's arms, but with her back-and-forth motion—something that apparently came standard-issue after giving birth, because Daisy did it too—and her cooing and patting, his wails turned to hiccups and occasional tears as he waited for his mom. Did that sway come to adoptive moms too? Or was it something you learned through the pregnancy-delivery process?

A high-pitched yelp came from a table—Paige's younger boy had apparently jumped off it and hurt his ankle when he landed. Paige returned Sorrel to Ilana's arms and rushed over, throwing a "Clean up that mess" at her older boy in a patient yet firm tone. Meanwhile, Sorrel's lungs refilled, and he screamed twice as loud as before.

Ilana wanted to cover her ears at the yowl that could surely shatter crystal, but she tried to copy what Paige had done with the rocking and patting and cooing. Nothing worked.

Paige had scooped the younger boy onto her lap and was inspecting his ankle. "It's okay, buddy," she said, rubbing it softly. "Now we know not to jump off tables, huh?"

Her son nodded miserably but gradually calmed down, tucking his head beneath her chin as Paige rocked and patted the toddler, calming him down just as she had Sorrel a minute before. At the table, her older son obediently stacked sugar packets back into the dish they'd been in—in nowhere near the same order as they belonged, but, hey, he was obedient—then scooped the salt and pepper into one pile at the center of the table, maybe so his mother could dispose of it. Ilana was impressed he hadn't just wiped it all onto the carpet.

Daisy finished shaking up the bottle and then, instead of taking the baby back, held the bottle out. Ilana stared at it as if the bottle might bite her.

"Want to feed him?" Daisy asked.

"I—guess so," Ilana lied. She took the bottle and sat on a chair, then tried to readjust the baby's position in her arms so she could feed him—the latter only made him wail the more. She touched the bottle's nipple to his mouth, and he immediately opened up, searching for food. She settled the bottle in his mouth, and he set to sucking away. His breathing eased, and his wails ended as quickly as they'd started, his eyes almost rolling with pleasure as he settled into Ilana's arms. Her lips curved into a small grin, which grew until it was a smile.

I did it! He'd calmed down in *her* arms. And she hadn't broken the baby either. This was as big a triumph as the huge Christmas expo she'd pulled off three years ago. She settled in with the baby, feeling more comfortable with the feel of him in her arms by the second.

Daisy sat on a nearby chair. "So tell us what's going on with you. How are things?"

Ilana glanced at the baby, remembering the envelope in her bag. Success at holding a bottle didn't necessarily equate with being a good mother. At first she felt too overwhelmed to say anything. Ilana replayed the last few minutes in her mind. Daisy hadn't been the least bit ruffled at her son's screams. And Paige had managed Sorrel as if she'd been born to be a mother. Plus, she'd handled her older, energetic boys with ease and grace. Ilana smiled and managed, "I'm hanging in there."

Am I up for any of this?

Sure, she'd known that babies cried and toddlers got into trouble and that motherhood wasn't all unicorns and glittering bubbles. But seeing motherhood in action with seasoned veterans handling it with nary a drop of sweat was something else. She knew full well that she would have probably yelled at her kids if they'd messed up a fancy restaurant table—and then jumped off it. She'd have blamed the kid for his own injury; it was his own stupid fault, right? Let him learn about gravity the hard way.

What if I get a colicky baby? Something that had once been a hypothetical "problem"—one she would have given her right arm to have and that she really had given years and tens of thousands of dollars toward—suddenly terrified her.

Motherhood was permanent and hard and . . . Ilana glanced at the tip of the tan envelope poking from the top of her bag. She should probably shred the documents for the sake of any children in the world unlucky enough to be placed with her. Or just drop the envelope over the side of the ship and get it over with.

I don't think I've got the right kind of mettle for this.

In rehab, one of her constant goals had been to face reality head on.

Yeah. Today, facing reality wasn't nearly what it was cracked up to be.

Little Sorrel finished the bottle and breathed deeply, having fallen asleep in Ilana's arms. She looked up at Daisy. "Now what?" she whispered, not wanting to wake him.

"Here, I'll burp him," Daisy said, reaching for her baby.

The moment Ilana handed him over, she felt an emptiness in her arms. She wanted to take him back, to snuggle the sweet newness of his little body—but she didn't know how to burp a baby, and she'd probably do it wrong.

Right then, Paige's younger boy came up to her. "I like your hair. It's curly," he proclaimed.

Ilana laughed. "It *is* curly," she acknowledged. "Do you wish you had curly hair?"

"Nah," he said with a shake of his head. "But Kailey in preschool has curly hair, and I think it's pretty." He grinned with the unashamed and unembarrassed confession of a child. "My foot still hurts. Can I sit on your lap?"

Taken aback, Ilana wasn't sure how to answer at first, but he was already hopping, trying to get up, so she grabbed under his arms and hoisted him onto her lap, where he leaned back and began sucking his thumb.

A warmth entered Ilana's chest, and she had to order her eyes to stop watering. Paige looked over at the two of them. "You're a natural," she said with a smile.

"I don't know about that," Ilana said. She still felt entirely inadequate and overwhelmed. There was so much to learn about babies and children that she didn't know what she didn't know.

But she'd fed a baby. And now a toddler was sitting on her lap of his own volition. Maybe she could figure out the rest. As she waited for the rest of the group to show up, she instinctively brushed his hair out of his eyes and began to rock from side to side.

Chapter 10
ATHENA
ANTICIPATION

ATHENA LOOKED OUT OVER THE balcony of the honeymoon suite she was booked into. It was all hers for now, but in just a few days she'd be sharing it with Grey. She'd been tempted to invite Grey inside after they'd checked in, but instead she'd kissed him at the door, then shut it between them. She was late for the book-club meeting, but she wanted a couple of moments to herself—to look out over the ocean and to inhale the sea air. She could almost smell Greece, they were so close.

As she thought about seeing her relatives, tears pricked her eyes. Some had come to the States for her mother's funeral last fall, but there were cousins in Greece she'd never met. They'd have dozens of questions about her father, of course, but hopefully Jackie would take care of most of those. It was still painful to think about neither of her parents being at her wedding.

The breeze tickled Athena's neck and pushed her short hair back. She'd had it highlighted and cut just below her ears right before coming. By her next hair appointment, she'd be a married woman. The diamond of her engagement ring sparkled in the sunlight, much like the tops of the cresting waves stretching before her.

Soon, she'd be Mrs. Ronning.

I'm ready. She had no doubts, no cold feet—just the warmth of gratitude. She wished her mother could see her now, could see the changed Athena. The humble Athena. The woman in love. Looking out into the endless blue, Athena decided her mother did know. And her mother did see.

Athena dabbed her eyes and turned away from the balcony. After closing the glass door, she grabbed her iPad and headed for the cabin door. When she stepped into the hall, a man leaning against a wall nearby cleared his throat.

"Grey! I said you couldn't come in. Not until after the wedding."

"I'm not *in* the room, am I?" He lifted his hands as if in surrender. "I just missed you."

Athena stepped into his arms. "You need to be stronger," she teased. "We can be apart for a few minutes, you know."

He pulled her close and pressed his lips against her neck. "I know, but for some reason my cell won't text. I wanted to tell you that I'll be up on deck with Andrew and the kids so you'll know where to find me when you're done with your meeting."

Now that she was in Grey's arms, she was reluctant to move away. "Have fun, Uncle Grey."

He laughed. "That sounds pretty official. Maybe I should come with you and stay in denial awhile longer."

Athena raised up on her toes and kissed him on the mouth, pulling away before it could deepen. "Nice try. I'll see you in about an hour."

Grey grabbed her hand as she moved away, but she twisted out of his grasp with a laugh. It would be good for him to spend time with Jackie's husband, Andrew, and their kids. Athena had spent plenty of time with Grey's siblings, so having the roles reversed on the cruise worked well. His brother, Jed, had come with his girlfriend, Lucy, but Grey's sisters hadn't been able to make the trip. And his mother had checked out from all family responsibility years ago.

On deck 10 forward, Athena found the restaurant they'd reserved. Laughter and a mixture of voices came through before she opened the door. Pushing through, she found that she was the last to arrive. Even Jackie was there, although she wasn't technically a member of the book club. The meeting was more about scheduling the next seven days than anything else.

"Athena!" Ruby said, stepping away from Daisy and her baby. "Come sit at the head of the table."

Athena smiled as she embraced Ruby. The book-club "mom" looked put together as always, wearing a red-and-white-striped top and white capris. Everything matched, down to her red-and-white slip-on shoes.

The others came forward to hug Athena too, Daisy with little Sorrel chewing on his fist, Paige with one of her boys hanging on her leg. Athena wasn't sure which one he was—they both looked the same, just in two sizes. Shannon smiled at her—she wasn't the huggy type—wearing a fun, bright-patterned dress, so different than the scrubs she usually wore. It seemed Shannon was really embracing the cruise spirit.

Ilana hugged her too, and Athena noted that the color was back in her face; she looked like she'd gained a few good, healthy pounds. Olivia was next—she always went for the extra-long hug. Olivia pulled back, looking stunning. She hadn't worn anything fancy, but her black blouse and sarong skirt fit nicely and made her look tall and elegant. Finally Victoria stepped forward, as gorgeous as ever.

"You're like a celebrity now," Athena said. "I'm so glad you could come with everything going on."

Victoria squeezed her tight. "I'm so sick of the media. I think I'll stay on this cruise for a year. Do you think they'll notice?"

Athena laughed. "Not if you keep changing your hairstyle and clothes."

With a sigh, Victoria said, "I wish it were that easy."

"Is everyone ready to start?" Ruby's voice rang out, always the organizer.

Athena walked to the table, passing her sister, Jackie, who reached out and squeezed her arm, a huge smile on her face.

At her sister's expression of obvious pride, Athena blinked back tears and sat at the head of the long table—well, a series of tables moved together. Seeing all these women together in one place, knowing they'd all come on this cruise for *her* . . . was overwhelming. "Wow. Thanks for coming, everyone." Her voice cracked. "I don't know what to say except that I'm so . . ." She took a deep breath before continuing. "I'm very touched that you're all here."

Ruby clapped her hands. "We're so happy for you and Grey. We wouldn't want to be anywhere else."

Athena laughed, and the other ladies joined in. Strangely enough, Athena wanted to hug them all again. Instead, she turned on her iPad and pulled up the memo app with her notes, which were coordinated with the ship's itinerary. "First, I'd like to thank Ruby for pulling this off—and Gabriel, of course, for finding us such a great deal."

The ladies broke into scattered clapping, and Ruby beamed.

"Basically, we want everyone to enjoy themselves and do whatever they want, but we do have a few things scheduled as a group . . . like the wedding." Athena found herself blushing as the ladies laughed. "It will be the day we make port in Athens. I've e-mailed you all the basic itinerary, but just know to be flexible." She met Jackie's knowing gaze. "My sister has done wonders with putting together the wedding, but Greeks can be passionate people, so if someone is unhappy, you may all hear about it."

Jackie just smiled.

"Do you need to warn them about anything specific?" Athena asked her.

Jackie looked around the table at all the women, meeting their curious gazes with confidence. "I have a few more details to finalize, and then I'll get everyone the full schedule. Just know that magical things happen in Greece."

The women fell quiet at Jackie's pronouncement.

"I agree," Ruby said, reaching over and patting Athena's hand. "Truer words were never spoken." Her face flushed, and Athena imagined that Ruby was remembering meeting Gabriel in Greece earlier that year. Athena thought it adorable that a woman of sixty-three had found the love of her life, even if Ruby wasn't about to admit it.

"I have a quick announcement," Ruby said, and everyone hushed again. "The bridal shower will be moved back an hour tomorrow night. That will give everyone more time to spend in Crete. Plus, some of you may be able to get your kids to bed beforehand."

"I told you not to worry about a shower," Athena said.

Ruby's smile was mischievous. "Too late. I already e-mailed everyone about it behind your back."

Athena's heart expanded. Since the loss of her mother, Athena had felt particularly close to Ruby. She'd become much more than a good friend.

"Do I dare ask if there is anything else to be discussed?" Athena said to Ruby.

"Just a few things," Ruby said with a chuckle, clasping her well-manicured hands. "Let's go around the table and make sure we have each other's room numbers. There are some places where cell phone service is spotty." When they'd all shared their room numbers, Ruby described some of the things they had to look forward to in Crete tomorrow. Then she turned to Jackie. "Do you have anything to add?"

Athena was pleased with how well Ruby and Jackie seemed to be working together on the wedding plans and the cruise as a whole. Ruby had been helpful yet not overbearing, and Jackie was more than competent.

Jackie gave a brief sketch of the timeline for the next few days and the small details leading up to the wedding.

Athena hadn't wanted a maid of honor or official bridesmaids. Instead, each of her book-club friends, as well as Jackie, would be honored equally. Jackie had ordered matching corsages for everyone. As Jackie spoke, Athena realized how much her sister was really doing while Athena was walking around all dreamy. She supposed that was the official right of all brides.

When Jackie finished and Ruby nodded her approval, Athena said, "Well, ladies. Thank you so much again. See you all at dinner."

Ruby stood and turned to Ilana, who'd been sitting next to her. "You and your husband should sit with Gabriel and me tonight."

Ilana nodded, but Athena didn't hear her response as everyone stood up from the table. The chatter in the room had grown, and Paige's two boys were playing some sort of airplane game, making zooming noises. Apparently their quiet behavior had reached its limit.

"Should we check on our men?" Jackie said, linking arms with Athena.

She liked the sound of that: *our men*. "Sure, unless you want to accidentally get lost somewhere near the spa."

"How long do you think it will be before they miss us?"

Athena thought about Grey waiting outside her room. "Our time may already be up."

She was sure Grey was having a good time, but she missed him already. It was kind of crazy to consider that less than a year ago she'd done everything to avoid a serious relationship with a man, and now . . . she was days from getting married. As bittersweet as it was to not have her mother or father here, this cruise was beyond anything she could have imagined.

Even if her father had been healthy enough to travel, he wouldn't have remembered anything, and it would have been horribly confusing to him as he moved in and out of lucidity.

They reached the main deck, which held an array of swimming pools and hot tubs—some designated for adults only, others for families.

Jackie's three kids were taking turns on a spiral waterslide that dumped into a crystal blue pool. Several other kids were in the pool as well, but it wasn't crowded.

"The kids are swimming?" Athena asked. She thought the kids would have at least waited until the next day, but apparently on a cruise the fun was not to be delayed.

On the far side of the pool, Andrew and Grey sat on lounge chairs, each holding a fancy drink in their hands while they watched the kids and talked to each other.

"Okay, those men are having way too much fun," Jackie said as the kids saw their mom and started calling to her.

"Watch me!" Jackie's six-year-old Maria yelled.

Jackie and Athena stopped and waited for Maria to go down the slide and splash into the pool. As soon as her niece hit the water, Athena moved toward Grey again.

"Wait," Jackie said, putting a restraining hand on Athena's arm. "If we aren't watching when Maria pops her head up, she'll think we weren't watching at all."

Athena waved to Maria when her head surfaced, and Maria beamed before swimming off, silently giving the women permission to shift their attention from her. Athena glanced around. "This place is like paradise. Good luck taking them home."

Jackie nodded. "You're telling me. The ship has activities all day long for the kids, and I don't even have to see them if I don't want to. Pretty tempting. Maybe Andrew and I can have a second honeymoon."

"This cruise is all about *me*, you know." Athena laughed.

Maria climbed out of the pool and ran straight for Jackie.

"Don't get me wet," Jackie said, taking a step back and patting Maria on top of her wet hair.

Within a couple of minutes the other two kids, eight-year-old Andy and four-year-old Eleni—wearing water wings—had climbed out of the water and run to their mother.

"Time to get dried off, I guess," Jackie said.

Athena followed the group over to the men. Andrew and Grey had jumped into action, helping the kids get their towels.

When Athena reached Grey, he slipped an arm around her waist and kissed her cheek.

"How was the meeting?" he asked over the noise of the kids chattering about how hungry they were.

"Great," she said. "I'm still amazed everyone came." She peered up at him. "How were the kids?"

He smiled. "Not a problem. I've totally got this."

"You can't go wrong with swimming," she said, feeling butterflies in her stomach at the way Grey was looking at her. She slid her hand into his, and they followed Jackie and the others past the collection of pools.

"Jed and Lucy wanted to meet for dinner. Are you all right with that?" Grey asked.

"Sounds good," Athena said. She'd always enjoyed the company of Grey's brother and sister-in-law.

Jackie, Andrew, and their kids left for their room, and Athena and Grey split off from the group to walk around the upper deck.

The blue-green water of the sea was stunning, turning darker as the sun moved toward the horizon. Athena leaned against the railing to look out over the sea, and Grey wrapped his arms around her from behind, resting his chin on her shoulder.

Athena closed her eyes against the breeze pushing through her hair. She felt as if she were a world away from every concern.

They were quiet like that for several moments, and then Grey said, "I think jet lag is kicking in. We should go take a nap."

Athena turned to face him, smiling. She wrapped her arms around his neck, and he leaned down, pulling her against him. "Only three more days, Mr. Ronning, and then we can take our naps together."

As Grey closed the distance to kiss her, her breath caught as she realized what she'd said. *Only three more days.*

Chapter 11

SHANNON
SEASICK

SHANNON HAD BEEN ON BOATS before, even a cruise ship not much different from this one, and had never had a problem with seasickness. She'd often counseled clients picking up medications prior to their own trips to start taking dimenhydrinate—Dramamine—a few days before the cruise to help them adjust to the medication's potential side effects of dizziness and nausea. By starting it before leaving on the trip, a person could be assured the medication was well within their system before it was needed—once someone was actually sick from the motion of the boat, it was much harder to treat. She ignored her own advice because she didn't have a history of motion sickness. Boy, was she regretting that now. The nausea hadn't come until dinner but had quickly descended into dizziness and overall bleck since then. She'd told her husband, John, and their son, Landon, to go to the show—a Broadway tribute—without her and found her way to the pharmacy that, while closed, had a box full of free antinausea pills. She'd taken a handful of packets, then staggered back to her room, where she'd taken two pills and collapsed on the bed in hopes of sleeping things off.

This morning—day two of their cruise—she'd rallied by telling herself that once she got on land she'd feel better. She bought some postcards from one of the shops at the pier but didn't feel well enough to do much more than that. She headed back to the cabin after assuring her men that she wanted them to stay and enjoy Crete. They had booked a tour to the Knossos ruins, and she made them promise to take lots of pictures before meeting her back on the ship for dinner. Hopefully she'd feel well enough to take an evening stroll through the quaint streets if she rested for the day.

She went back to bed and woke up feeling well enough to see if some toast would take the edge off her hunger. On her way out of the room, she grabbed the postcards in hopes of filling them out in time to have them mailed from the island rather than the ship, which didn't seem nearly as cool.

Only the Paradise Buffet was open while they were in port, so Shannon grabbed an English muffin, ordered a ginger ale from the bar—for three dollars, thank you very much—and found a table on the deck where she could at least *look* at the island of Crete. It was beautiful with its narrow streets winding through multicolored square buildings built upon the hillsides. The blue water surrounding the pier was nothing like the Pacific Ocean Shannon knew, and she allowed herself to get lost in the colors and textures and visual tapestry in front of her. *Where are John and Landon right now?* She took a bite of bread while trying not to feel sorry for herself. Determined not to hold a pity party for one, she turned her attention to the postcards. The pictures were of different views of the island, not much different from the view she had right now.

Writing a few sentences about their trip so far—minus the seasickness—to her parents and John's parents was easy. It was the third postcard that caused her to tap her pen on the table as she regarded it. Keisha, her stepdaughter, had been sentenced to 120 days of mandatory rehab after her arrest last May, with the option of staying for six months at the expense of the state if she chose to. Shannon and John had encouraged her to take all the help she could get, but three weeks ago they'd learned Keisha had chosen to leave after 120 days. Shannon and John were so disappointed, and even more so when Shannon realized the shortened stay meant Keisha would get released while they were gone on this trip. A few dozen Al-Anon classes weren't enough to keep Shannon from considering backing out of the cruise altogether. She knew Keisha would need help getting settled, that bad habits and bad people would be waiting to welcome her back to the world she'd left against her will when she'd been arrested. Shannon also felt guilty for taking a vacation at such a precarious time.

A candid discussion with John, advice from the therapist who the family had been seeing, and her own better judgment eventually helped her remember the boundaries she'd already set and the reason for those boundaries in the first place. Chief among them was that she needed to see Keisha as an adult rather than a little girl. Being able to realize that had clearly been a "win" for Shannon's growth, but like a recovering alcoholic, Shannon longed for her own kind of drink: helping Keisha out, making things easier for her, feeling secure in Keisha's need for her. Was sending a postcard to make sure Keisha knew she was thinking about her and wanting to help her a good or bad thing? Would sending this postcard be the first step to being pulled back into Keisha's problems?

"Mind if I join you?"

Shannon looked up to see Daisy pushing a stroller. Baby Sorrel was sleeping like . . . well, a baby. "Not at all," Shannon said, waving toward the empty chair on the other side of the table and putting down her pen. "You didn't go into port?"

"We did." Daisy sat down and looked out at Crete. She let out a breath that reflected Shannon's own frustration of being on the ship when such beauty lay before them. "I managed to buy a gorgeous sundress at one of the shops before the stowaway hit his limit. Why are you here?"

Shannon related her seasickness story.

"That's so not fair," Daisy said. "Did you try the bracelet?" Daisy lifted her wrist, showing a rather unattractive gray wristband like the sweatbands people wore when they played basketball—Shannon had seen them before and didn't believe they had one ounce of scientific proof to recommend them. "I know—it's hideous," Daisy said, frowning at it. "And I can't tell you why it works, but I'm a believer. The last time I was on a cruise I was sick as a dog until a sweet Chinese lady gave me one of her bands. Saved my life, I swear. You can buy them at the gift shop on the boat."

"That's good to know," Shannon said without committing to the idea. She knew the explanation on the bracelet's effectiveness was based on acupuncture and things of that nature, but she suspected it was mostly a placebo effect that wouldn't work on her since she was already questioning its potential.

"So not fair," Daisy said again, shaking her head as she too looked over the island. "We should be out there . . . doing . . ." She turned back to Shannon. "What do people do in Greece?"

"Um, sing with Pierce Brosnan?"

Daisy made a face. "Can't we just look at him? And maybe have him read the back of cereal boxes so we can listen to that fabulous voice—it wouldn't matter what he said, really. That's all I'd need to be happy."

Shannon laughed, and for the next half an hour she and Daisy talked about their families and work. It was the first real conversation Shannon had ever had with Daisy; her pregnancy and new baby had kept her away from most of the book groups Shannon had attended. They'd had the same flight but hadn't sat close to one another—though Shannon had felt for Daisy when Sorrel had started screaming.

Daisy nodded toward the postcards on the table in front of Shannon. "I meant to pick one of those up for my folks but completely forgot. Maybe we'll go back out after his nap."

Shannon looked at the blank postcard intended for Keisha. "Want this one?"

"Oh no," Daisy said, shaking her head. "It's yours. You certainly had someone in mind when you bought it."

"Well, yeah, but I'm not sure what to say or if I should send it at all. Heck, I don't even know *where* to send it."

Daisy pulled her eyebrows together, and Shannon took a breath, feeling nervous to talk about Keisha out loud and yet wanting to share, which she took as a sign of how much had changed for her in past months—she was no longer holding in all her thoughts.

"It's for Keisha," Shannon finally said as though revealing a deep, dark secret. She'd updated the book group about Keisha's court-ordered rehab a couple of months ago—Daisy had been there. "She gets out of jail on Wednesday, but I don't know where she'll go or who she'll be staying with."

Daisy paused, and Sorrel started fussing in his stroller. "As in *this* Wednesday?" She bent over to put the pacifier in the baby's mouth. A moment later it bobbed up and down, and the baby was asleep again. "Two days from now, while we're on the boat?"

Shannon nodded, trying not to feel judged, even though she knew *she* was judging herself more harshly than anyone else would. She braced herself for Daisy's response, which would surely have judgment in it somewhere, right? If it did, would that make Shannon feel better about reaching out toward Keisha?

"No wonder you're sick."

Shannon blinked. "What?"

"The whole physical-emotional connection. Didn't you say you hadn't been sick on ships before? I bet the stress is making your body use this as an excuse to physically feel what your heart's going through."

Shannon didn't buy into that Eastern Zen stuff any more than she did bracelets that calmed someone's stomach . . . yet she *hadn't* been sick on other cruises. Just this one. She looked at Daisy's bracelet again, then glanced at a table not far from there, where two other people had bracelets on their wrists. Did *everything* have to have a scientific explanation to be true? It was a startling realization, and Shannon felt her defenses weaken as she sincerely considered Daisy's suggestion. "You really think so?"

Daisy shrugged and gave a sheepish grin. "I don't know, really, but it's something I've looked into. A friend of mine suggested the possibility when I had so many complications with this little guy." She glanced at the stroller, and her smile changed to one of tenderness before she looked at Shannon. "There was so much turmoil going on in my life, what with my husband and my own expectations and things. It made a lot of sense to me that my body was kind of forcing me to do less, to think more about what my body was really doing, and deal with my emotional stress. I read some books about it, and it kind of spurred me to work through things differently—better." She paused, and her eyes went wide as her cheeks flushed. "Not that I'm telling you you need to work things through like I did."

Shannon smiled, not the least bit offended. "I definitely need to change my head," she said, encouraged by Daisy's willingness to talk about her own struggles. "It's ridiculous how . . . *guilty* I feel about being here. Even though I have all these boundaries in place and know I won't fall into the same enabling behaviors I got wrapped up in before, I feel like I should be there in case Keisha wants to talk. I feel like I should be available. Instead, I'm halfway around the world."

"And if you feel so sick that you don't enjoy yourself, you have less to feel guilty about."

The idea washed over Shannon like the waves gently lapping the rocks that surrounded the island. "Oh my gosh," she said under her breath. "That makes such a pathetic amount of sense."

Daisy looked a bit uncomfortable. "Or maybe I just talk too much."

"No, no," Shannon said with a laugh. "You're brilliant, and you're right—there's a part of me that would feel better about not being there if I don't have a good time here. Gosh, that's twisted." Saying it aloud was like seeing what was hiding behind door three. *This* truth hit all the same chords other truths had hit for months as Shannon learned a lot of hard things about herself.

"I think it's sweet that you worry about her, though," Daisy said. The baby fussed again, so she rolled the stroller back and forth a few inches as if trying to rock him back to sleep. "I hope one day Keisha realizes how lucky she is to have you. Remember when we read *The Glass Castle*? The fact that any of those kids rose out of the lives their parents created for them is inspiring—and the author did it without anyone to support her. You being in Keisha's life will always give her that much more hope that she can beat this. That's amazing."

"I hope so," Shannon said. "But I still have so much to learn about how to be in her life without letting her take over mine. I'm really nervous about it."

For another thirty minutes they talked in depth about Keisha's history and Shannon's fears. Through it all, in the back of her mind Shannon marveled that she could be this open with anyone, let alone Daisy, who, until now, was one of the book-group ladies she knew the least. Daisy didn't heap advice or put Keisha down; she just made comments and talked about a friend whose son had struggled for years before taking accountability. Being so open with someone was refreshing.

The conversation had turned to Athena's wedding when Daisy's phone chimed from the diaper bag slung over the back of the stroller. She retrieved it, and her face lit up as she checked the text message. "It's Stormy and Jared at the fortress," she said, turning the phone to show Daisy a picture someone had taken of a good-looking man and Daisy's petite daughter making muscle-man poses in front of the ancient fort.

"That's adorable," Shannon said after Daisy turned the phone around and started typing a response. "It's sure sweet that Jared came with you to help take care of the baby."

Daisy looked at Shannon over her phone, her eyes narrowed just enough to be noticeable. Her expression tightened. "Not you too."

"Me too what?" Shannon didn't know what she'd said, so she reviewed the conversation in her mind but couldn't figure out what she'd said that had triggered Daisy's defenses.

Daisy must have read her expression, because hers softened as she shook her head. "Sorry, I'm paranoid."

"And I have no idea what you're talking about. Paranoid about what?"

Daisy gave her an indulgent look. "I'm sure you and the other ladies have talked about the fact that my *ex*-husband volunteered to come on this cruise with me."

"Ruby said he came because the cruise was a graduation trip for Stormy." Shannon didn't see any cause for a paranoia factor in that either.

"Really? You haven't been involved in gossipy comments about him and me and . . ."

Shannon's eyebrows rose. "You and he are *together*?"

"No!" Daisy said, her cheeks flaming. "We totally aren't, but I get how it looks and stuff, and Stormy keeps teasing me about it, and Tori made a comment about it at book group, and . . . Sheesh, forget I said anything."

Shannon regarded her newish friend, who was suddenly removing a bottle and premeasured formula packet from the diaper bag even though the baby was sound asleep. The tense moment was similar to what Shannon had had with Aunt Ruby a few months ago when the woman had refused to admit any feelings for Gabriel. "I wasn't at that book group," Shannon said.

Daisy shook the bottle. "Oh."

The silence got a little awkward, spurring Shannon to attempt a rescue. "What do you think about our families having dinner together one of these nights?" Shannon asked in an attempt to break the tension and change the subject. "I'd love to meet your daughter—I've heard so much about her from Paige. I know Landon is younger than Stormy, but she's the only other teenager in our group, and maybe they'll hit it off too."

Daisy softened over the course of a few thoughtful seconds. "That would be great. I've been a little surprised how little I've seen of the book-group ladies so far. I thought we'd be eating all our meals together or something."

"Me too," Shannon agreed. "Smaller groups are easier to get to know people, though—the idea of a meal with all the ladies and their families is a little daunting."

"Do you have plans for tonight? Jared and Stormy are coming back in time for dinner, but maybe your husband and son are staying on Crete longer."

Shannon shook her head. "They were coming back for dinner on the ship. Then, if I'm feeling better, we talked about going to the island for some gelato or something before the ship leaves port."

"Then tonight would be perfect," Daisy said. The baby started to whimper and this time spit out his pacifier and blinked open his eyes. Daisy expertly unbuckled him and lifted him out of the stroller while making cooing comments about him being a hungry boy. The bottle was ready to go, and he began sucking as soon as the nipple entered his mouth. He molded into his mother, and Shannon couldn't help but smile at the sweet picture the two of them created. Seeing them now, no one would have guessed that when Daisy found out she was pregnant she hadn't wanted another baby.

After a minute, Daisy looked up at Shannon with a hesitant expression. "You won't tease me about Jared?"

"Promise," Shannon said, drawing a cross over her heart.

"No one talked to you about Jared and me? Really?"

"Nope," Shannon said with a laugh. "Are you a little disappointed that you're not the hot gossip?" She kept it to herself that she hadn't seen much of the other women anyway. Even Aunt Ruby, someone Shannon assumed would be hovering, had been strangely removed—hopefully because she was making out with Gabriel. The idea made Shannon smile even wider.

"I don't want to be the subject of gossip," Daisy finally said in a somewhat lame attempt to explain.

"But you *would* like to know what people think?" Shannon said, phrasing the statement like a question in hopes the delivery would feel softer.

Daisy didn't answer at all this time; instead she watched Sorrel suck on his bottle.

"Want to know what I think?" Shannon asked, feeling braver and leaning across the table.

Daisy looked up, seemingly willing to hear Shannon's thoughts on the matter. Shannon liked that she seemed to have Daisy's trust. Shannon didn't consider herself a natural at reading people, but the hints Daisy had sent weren't that subtle, and Shannon felt sure that Daisy was looking for a little encouragement. "I think Jared sounds like a really great guy."

"He is," Daisy said, her whole body relaxing.

"He must think really highly of you too, to agree to a trip like this."

Daisy looked back at her baby without responding, but her expression was thoughtful.

"And," Shannon said, causing Daisy to look at her again, "Jackie says magical things happen in Greece."

Daisy stiffened, so Shannon hurried to speak before Daisy could shut her down. "I'm not saying anything *will* happen, and I know *you* know that if something were to spark between you two that you'd have to be careful and hyperaware of the impact a relationship could make, but I'd also hate for you to miss out on some of that magic just because you dismiss the idea out of hand. He *did* come on this cruise with you, and Ruby told me how fabulous he's been the last several months."

"It seems like such a can of worms," Daisy said, sounding fearful. "What if we tried something and it didn't work? What would that mean to Stormy?"

Shannon shrugged. "What if you tried something and it *did* work? What would *that* mean to Stormy? And to Sorrel? And to you? Being in love is wonderful, Daisy, and while I know you've had your share of heartbreak, that doesn't mean you can't find something fabulous—no matter what he may have been to you before."

"I can't think that way," Daisy said, shaking her head. "Gosh, what if he hasn't thought about this at all, and I'm stressing about something that isn't even on his radar? We're divorced. It didn't work the first time, so why would it work now?"

"Honestly?" Shannon said. "I don't think you would be stressing about this if you didn't think it *was* on his radar, and I don't think he'd be here helping you if he didn't want to be. You know he could have more easily *not* come on this trip with *your* friends and *your* baby. But he's here, as equally focused on you and your baby as he is on Stormy. That says a lot."

Daisy blinked, then slumped against her chair as though the conversation had worn her out. "Wow." She closed her eyes and looked truly terrified at her own realizations.

"I have an idea," Shannon said, scooting forward a little in her chair as the excitement began to build. "After dinner, why don't the four of us grown-ups—and Sorrel if you don't feel like you can leave him behind—go for gelato and leave the kids on the ship—it won't be for long. The bridal shower isn't until 9:00 p.m. We can make it back by then. John and I are easygoing, so we won't put you guys on the spot or anything, but maybe it will give you a chance to see Jared a little differently, and vice versa."

"What if you're not feeling good enough?"

"I'll make *sure* I feel better." Shannon noted that she felt better than she had this morning.

Daisy had a lot to think about, and Shannon gave her several seconds before Daisy agreed that it sounded like a lot of fun.

"I think I'll head back to my cabin and try to get another nap in before dinner," Shannon said, standing and putting her napkin over her plate. "And I'm going to pick up one of those bracelets on the way."

Daisy smiled up at her. "I'm glad I found you out here. I'll confirm dinner after Jared and Stormy get back. If you don't feel up to it, we'll put it off to another night."

"Do you want me to help you get back to your room with Sorrel? I feel bad leaving you here by yourself."

"I'd like to look over the island a little longer," Daisy said, nodding toward the city both of them had seen mostly from a distance. "And I've got a lot to think about."

Shannon insisted Daisy keep the third postcard and send it to her parents—it might be best for Shannon not to write Keisha until she better knew her motivations to do so—and they made their good-byes.

On her way back to the room, Shannon reflected on the challenges Daisy had dealt with in recent months—an unexpected pregnancy, the crumbling of her marriage, her daughter moving in with her dad, a move, bed rest, a new baby. And now feelings developing between her and her ex-husband. Shannon couldn't imagine what all of that must feel like, yet Daisy was embracing motherhood, taking all the changes in stride, and possibly exploring things with Jared, at least a little.

Thinking of Daisy caused Shannon to think of Ilana and all she'd dealt with this summer. Having played a small part in Ilana's situation last spring, and the fact that Ilana's problems so closely resembled Keisha's, Shannon's heart softened even more. Ilana was still struggling—Shannon could see it in the tightness of her expression at the wedding-planning meeting yesterday—but she was working every day to be better and had come on a cruise that had complimentary drinks and a full-service bar, despite how hard that must be to resist.

Aunt Ruby had worked through her hesitations to build a relationship with Gabriel, and Tori had risked her career to follow her heart. In fact, every woman in the book group had dealt with hard things since Shannon had met them. Some had made it through their darkness to the light on the other side, but some, like Ilana and Paige, and maybe even Ruby, were still waiting for the sun to come out completely and dry up all that rain.

Shannon bought the bracelet and put it on before she even left the store. On her way to her room, she noticed how many people were wearing them—they must work if so many people thought so; science schmience. The steward had made up the room in her absence, and Shannon pulled the heavy curtains over the porthole, plunging the room into darkness. A minute later, she snuggled into the comforter, hopeful that when she woke up she'd feel good as new. She was still worried about Keisha but was beginning to think that being on a floating city in the middle of the Mediterranean was probably the best place she could be when Keisha faced the world again. Shannon was surrounded by strong women facing hard things, not all of which could be resolved in a few months, or even years. But they were all doing their best. Shannon had a fabulous support system in these women and in her family.

She could do her best and get stronger too.

Chapter 12
RUBY
THE PERFECT MAN

RUBY BREATHED IN THE WARM, salty air. There was really nothing quite like Mediterranean Sea air on a warm day. She stood in the middle of the Crete bazaar while Gabriel haggled over the price of a gorgeous leather purse, which was as soft as a baby's cheek. Ruby had been inspecting it for only a few seconds when the shop owner had begun a pushy sales pitch.

Gabriel met Ruby's gaze, questioning, *Do you like it?* Ruby gave a slight nod. That was all it took. He wasn't about to let the shop owner get away with offering the top-dollar tourist price. Gabriel had spent most of the previous year working as a tour guide on the mainland, so he was no stranger to bazaars and haggling. When Gabriel started speaking Greek, the shop owner was quick to back down. Ruby wasn't sure of the final price because the men finished bargaining entirely in Greek.

"So . . ." she said to a beaming Gabriel as they walked away from the flustered shop owner.

Gabriel handed over the sack containing the purse, and she laughed as she opened it to peer inside. "Thank you! How much did he lose?"

"He still made about ten percent," Gabriel said. "He'll make it up within the hour."

"I'd better keep my bargain man a secret or all the ladies will want you as their shopping partner." Ruby was jostled by a group of young kids selling glass bead bracelets with evil eyes.

Gabriel slipped his hand into hers, keeping her close and dodging animated merchants as they made their way through the crowd. "The key is to not let on that you're a tourist."

"What are you saying?" Ruby asked, touching the tip of her large straw hat. The pale pink matched perfectly with her pink-Gingham blouse and dark-pink rimmed sunglasses.

"That you look like a beautiful tourist," Gabriel said, slowing and placing a kiss on her cheek.

Ruby was sure her face was now as pink as her hat. How did he make her do that? A kiss on the cheek in a crowded bazaar and suddenly she wanted to sit down in the shade and cool off. Jackie's statement from the previous night came to mind: *Magical things happen in Greece.*

Since meeting Gabriel in Greece last spring, Ruby definitely agreed. Going on that two-week tour with her friends from the senior center had been a healing circle, one Ruby hadn't fully understood herself until months later. Her *first* tour to Greece had been when she'd discovered her late husband's unfaithfulness, but on her second tour thirty years later, she'd met Gabriel . . . and had found a second chance at love.

Ruby's cheeks flushed at her thoughts. Yes, she loved Gabriel, and she'd even been brave enough to tell him so after he told her first. But like all things in their relationship, he seemed more comfortable moving at a faster pace than she did.

I'm not getting any younger, but I want to take things slow, Ruby thought and let out a small sigh.

"What was that sigh for?" Gabriel said, tugging her out of the way of a particularly aggressive vendor selling gold chains and silk scarves.

He even noticed her sighs. "Just thinking how lucky I am. Thanks for getting me the purse." This time she slowed and kissed *his* cheek.

Gabriel chuckled, moving his hand around her waist and pulling her into a hug. "Anytime."

Ruby believed it. Gabriel was always there for her—always true and dependable. After both of their disastrous marriages, it was a miracle they'd found each other. They started walking again, and Ruby appreciated that the sun was starting to sink into the horizon. The lowering sun took the edge off the heat, although it meant a full day had almost passed on the cruise. She felt as if she was already running out of time to prepare for Athena's wedding. There were still final details to go over with Jackie, but she could do nothing about that until they returned to the ship.

So Ruby determined to stay in the moment and enjoy every bit of it on Crete.

"I know a great place to eat on the harbor," Gabriel said. "It will get us out of this crowd."

"Sounds great." The throng seemed to increase by the second, and Ruby suspected that the tourists had finished visiting sights and were now making final purchases before returning to their ships.

They left the bazaar and turned into a narrow alley that opened up onto the harbor. Seagulls flew overhead, calling to each other. A few feet ahead a small girl sat on the edge of the dock, holding out crackers to the birds, then tossing the crackers as far as she could. The scavengers swooped closer as she teased them. The girl's dark, braided hair and white sundress complemented the turquoise sky and myriad of sailboats bobbing in the harbor. It was a picture-worthy scene.

Ruby and Gabriel continued past the girl, smiling at her antics. They'd reached a row of outdoor cafés when someone called out.

"Ruby?"

A young couple sat at a table, both wearing hats and sunglasses, so it took a moment for Ruby to realize it was Tori and Christopher, who both stood to greet them. Tori hugged Ruby, and Chris and Gabriel shook hands.

"Would you like to join us?" Tori asked.

Ruby glanced at Gabriel, and he seemed to approve. "We'd love to," she said. They sat across from the young couple. "I almost didn't recognize you," Ruby told Tori.

"That's the point." Tori adjusted her enormous sunglasses.

"But you're in Crete, dear," Ruby said. "Would the media catch on way over here?" Granted, they were a striking couple, but people in Europe would probably think they were a pair of models.

"You'd be surprised at how far Hollywood media reaches," Christopher said, sliding over a magazine tabloid. It was in Greek, but the cover had a picture of Christopher grinning and looking debonair and a picture of Tori with a frown, standing by a car.

"When was this?" Ruby asked.

"Oh," Tori said with a wave of her hand. "The day we found out about the cruise. Someone wrote a nasty message on my car. I didn't even notice the photographer. He must have had one of those high-zoom lenses."

Ruby didn't need the headlines interpreted to know it was negative toward Tori. She was plainly depicted as the sour-faced fiancée. Having watched *Vows* from the moment she knew Tori was on the production staff, Ruby knew a lot of fans, as well as the studio, were upset with Christopher's choice. Ruby reached over and patted Tori's hand. "You're a brave woman. Ignore the media. They don't know the real you."

"That's what Chris keeps telling me," Tori said, leaning against him. He slid his arm around her, looking more than pleased to be able to do so.

"Don't worry; we won't blow your cover," Gabriel said, and everyone laughed.

A waiter brought out a couple more menus, but Ruby asked Gabriel to order for her. She loved listening to him speak Greek, and Christopher's Southern accent was charming as well. It seemed that she and Tori had landed the most handsome men on the cruise. She chuckled at her own thoughts, and when everyone looked at her, she waved a hand. "Oh, don't mind me. I'm just enjoying myself."

"It's the purse," Gabriel said, holding up the sack.

Tori inspected it, oohing over the soft leather.

"Do you want one, babe?" Christopher asked Tori, and the way she smiled at him was adorable. Young love was so sweet.

"I'm good just sitting here with you . . . away from the masses," Tori said.

Christopher grinned. Gabriel leaned back and draped an arm across Ruby's chair. She inhaled his masculine scent, and her stomach fluttered. Not-so-young love was pretty great too.

By the time their food came, Ruby was starving. Gabriel had ordered her some sort of chopped salad with lamb chunks and a yogurt dressing. It was delicious—cool and crisp to offset the warm, spicy meat.

They spent the next hour together talking and laughing over Tori and Christopher's adventures in becoming professional media-dodgers. Then Christopher turned to some of his experiences on set during filming. "I tried like crazy to get Tori's attention, but she avoided me as much as she could."

Tori laughed. "For the first week I had a horrible cold and could hardly stand to be around myself. And by the second week I knew it was dangerous to spend time with a heartbreaker like Christopher."

"I'm not a heartbreaker," he protested, tugging her toward him.

Tori squirmed away with a laugh. "You are the *worst* heartbreaker." She shoved the tabloid at him, but he pushed it aside and pulled her in for a kiss. Soon they were both laughing.

Ruby smiled, feeling a bit teary eyed at the realization that she had no idea what it was like to be truly in love at Tori's age. The young couple was blessed indeed to have found each other soon enough to have so many years left to enjoy together.

"Sorry," Tori said, settling against Christopher and looking at Ruby. "We can be obnoxious sometimes."

"You're fine," Ruby said. "I'm glad you were able to get away for the cruise."

"Me too," Christopher said. He stood and helped Tori to her feet. "We should be getting back to the ship."

"Yeah, I still need to wrap Athena's shower gift," Tori said. "Are you guys coming, or do you have more shopping to do?"

Before Ruby could answer, Gabriel said, "We have one more stop."

She looked at him in surprise but didn't want to question him in front of the others. Tori leaned down for a hug, and Ruby patted her on the back.

"See y'all later," Christopher said. He leaned over and hugged Ruby as well.

When they were alone, Gabriel reached for Ruby's hand and lifted it to his lips to press a kiss on it.

"Well, Mr. Alexakis, what's this 'one more stop'? More bargaining?"

Gabriel squeezed her hand. "There's a place I want to show you. You'll love it."

Ruby let him lead her out of the group of tables. They walked along the harbor, then turned up a road leading away from the center of town. Gabriel pointed out a few sights on their way up a gradual hill. She liked having her own personal tour guide.

The sun had settled on the horizon, casting a golden glow on everything and causing the brilliant white buildings to mellow into a soft yellow.

This part of town was much quieter than the bazaar, and it had a calm, peaceful feeling. The air had cooled, and Ruby was grateful for the reprieve. She wanted to take off her hat but feared horrible hat hair, so she judiciously left it on.

"Almost there," Gabriel said, turning up a narrow lane.

They walked along a hedged path with all kinds of floral fragrances floating around them. A moment later the path opened into a neat courtyard surrounded by trimmed bushes and blooming plants. At the end of the courtyard stood an ancient archway leading to an even older church. The island had dozens of churches. This one was whitewashed, and with the surrounding foliage so well groomed the place had an almost fairy-tale-like feel.

"What a gorgeous little hideaway," Ruby said. "What church is this?"

"It's one of St. Mary's churches. The locals call it *Parádeisos Ekklisía*—Paradise Church."

"I can see why. It's beautiful." Ruby noticed a small table with a bottle of wine and goblets inside the arch. "Some sort of religious offering?"

"No," Gabriel said, his fingers grasping hers. "Something for us."

Ruby chuckled with surprise. "What are you up to?"

He said nothing as he led her to the arch. Once beneath it, he stopped, taking her other hand so that they faced each other.

Ruby's breath caught as she looked at the man across from her. She didn't know why she suddenly felt so nervous. Obviously this was something Gabriel had planned . . . on Crete, no less. She wanted to ask a dozen questions, but something told her to wait.

"I arranged for the wine because I hoped we'd have something to celebrate."

Warmth spread along the back of Ruby's neck as Gabriel's brown eyes held hers. She nodded for him to continue; she didn't know if she could speak properly. If her thudding heart was any indication, he was about to ask . . .

"Ruby, when you showed up in Greece six months ago, I didn't know that my life would change forever," he said in a quiet voice. "I didn't know that you would be the woman who would save me from despair, the woman who would make me into the man I hoped to become one day."

Tears burned Ruby's eyes. She could say all of the same things about him. He'd saved her . . . he'd showed her that a broken heart didn't have to stay broken.

"When I realized I was falling in love with you, I knew I'd never be the same. I left the old Gabriel behind, and I never want to go back to him. We're getting on in years, but I think we have a good twenty or thirty left, and I want to spend every minute of them with you." He took a small step closer and lowered his voice. "I don't want to be sent home at night anymore."

She smiled through threatening tears. She didn't want to send him home at night either, but taking things to the next step was beyond her ability right now. Things were perfect how they were. Couldn't he see that? He'd fixed the break in her heart, but there were still many cracks.

Gabriel released her hands and knelt on the paved stone.

Ruby brought a hand to her mouth. He was really doing it. Her emotions swirled inside of her.

He pulled out a small box from his pocket and opened the lid. Inside was a diamond ring encircled by scarlet gems—rubies.

"Gabriel," she whispered, her pulse racing. There was no turning back from this—he was changing the level of their relationship. But she didn't know if she could accept his proposal, no matter how much she loved him. Fear pulsed through her at the thought of entering into a commitment that could wreck her heart yet again. "I—"

"Ruby," he interrupted, his gaze holding hers. "I'm not asking you to marry me."

"You're—you're not?" The fear diminished, but her heart beat erratically with nervousness all the same.

"I'm asking you to think about it," he said. "To take this ring, and when I see you wearing it, I'll know you're ready to become Mrs. Alexakis. Even if it takes a year or two or a decade, I'll understand. But I don't want you to have any doubt of what I'm hoping in my heart."

Tears trickled down her cheeks as she stared at him. He was proposing but without demanding an answer. He was promising himself to her, and he was willing to wait for her to return that promise.

She took a steadying breath. She couldn't imagine saying no to such an honorable request. But to *marry* again? "All right." Her voice caught. "I'll take the ring and keep it safe."

Gabriel rose and set the ring in the palm of her hand. She closed her fingers around it and threw her arms around his neck. Gabriel pulled her tightly against him, and Ruby let herself melt. He was perfect; this was perfect. She wanted to sit and sob because he understood her and knew what she needed. He wouldn't rush her; he'd stand by, waiting until she could completely give herself to him.

"I love you," she whispered.

He drew away and kissed her, then whispered back, "I love you too."

Chapter 13

PAIGE
100 PERCENT

AFTER SPENDING A FEW HOURS ashore at the Kusadasi port in Ephesus, Turkey, on their fourth day of the cruise, Paige's boys had worn themselves out, so she returned to the ship. They rested for about an hour, at which point they were eager for more fun, so she took them to the pool. She found a shady spot next to where Daisy had stretched out, then settled in to watch as the boys splashed each other and giggled out of control. From her reclined deck chair, Paige reached for her bag and pulled out her digital camera, then snapped several shots of the moment. The past few days had flown by; she could hardly believe the cruise was half over.

Daisy held Sorrel on her lap beside Paige, taking pictures of him with her smartphone. "You need one of these," Daisy said, waving her phone before tucking it into her bag and snuggling her baby. "Getting the pictures off is so much easier from a phone."

"I'll have to take your word for it." Paige had to admit that she coveted everyone's smartphones and couldn't wait for the day—and she liked to assume it would arrive soon—that she could afford one.

Nate ran out of the water and threw his dripping arms around his mother. Paige sucked in a breath at the sudden cold, then held him at a distance with one arm, keeping her other out to the side so the camera wouldn't get wet.

"Having fun?" Paige asked, pulling back.

"It's *awesome*," Nate said with wide eyes. "Watch me, Mommy!"

And he was off again. This time he did an elaborate belly flop, then showed off his "alligator" walk with his hands in the shallow end. Paige made sure she watched the entire time and nodded and commented as needed until Nate got distracted by Shawn and the two began playing together.

Paige sighed with contentment. So far the trip had been amazing. Each of the ports had something different to offer, and while her boys were unlikely to remember much about the sights when they got older, she had photographic proof that they'd seen some of the great historical landmarks and had eaten in pretty fantastic places.

That is, I'll have evidence if I can keep the boys from destroying the camera, she thought as she tucked it back into her bag.

Ilana and Ethan appeared in their swimsuits and greeted Daisy and Paige. Ethan had his arm around Ilana's shoulders. When they stopped at some empty deck chairs a few yards down, she kissed his cheek—or probably meant to, but he was tall enough that she reached only his jawline. He turned to return the kiss full on the lips. Paige watched them longingly, wishing she had someone to care for her and love her like that. Someone kind and gentle like Derryl . . .

She cleared her throat and looked away, feeling like an intruder, even though their PDA was right out in the open. She pretended to read her book but surreptitiously watched as Ethan rubbed sunscreen on Ilana's back and arms.

Good thing my sunglasses are dark, Paige thought. No one would be able to tell she was watching them.

Daisy continued cooing to her baby, not noticing Paige's distraction. But both women looked up at the sound of a familiar, bright voice.

"Well, now, there you are," Ruby said. This would have been where she normally greeted them with one of her crushing hugs, but she was holding Gabriel's hand instead.

After popping Sorrel's pacifier into his mouth, Daisy said, "Were you looking for us?"

Gabriel smiled. "Just hoping to find a chance to get us all together for a meal."

With an emphatic nod, Ruby agreed. "It's so easy to go along, day after day, and not even see one another," she said. "Do you two have plans for tonight? If not, shall we save tables for the group?"

Paige found herself nodding as Daisy spoke for them both. "Please do. Dinner together would be great." She indicated the Goldbergs farther down. "You can tell Ilana and Ethan right now too. They're over there."

"Oh, wonderful," Ruby said, her shoulders rising and falling with excitement. "Say six o'clock at the Grand Dining Room?"

Before Paige or Daisy could answer Ruby, the older couple—totally twitterpated and glowing with newfound love—were walking toward Ilana and Ethan.

The pang of loneliness grew stronger inside Paige. So help her, if Athena and Grey showed up, or Tori and Chris—both couples always lost in each other's eyes—Paige would throw up. No, that wasn't right. Seeing them all lost in romance didn't make her ill; it made her envious. She'd give a lot to have the same thing.

Last month marked a year since the divorce was final. And eight months since she'd broken up with Derryl.

Why did I do that, again?

As soon as the question crossed her mind, she chastised herself. She knew full well why. She'd married the first boyfriend she'd ever had and had never gained the life experience or independence she'd needed to mother her boys. Jumping from one relationship into another wasn't wise. She couldn't go rebounding—although she hated thinking of Derryl as a rebound. She'd needed time and space. She'd needed to find out who Paige was under all the other labels she'd worn over the years.

The last eight months had been very good in that regard. She felt better, stronger, more confident. Happier.

Except at times like this.

"I'm the only single person in a sea of couples," she muttered.

"What?" Daisy glanced over from her baby-adoring.

Paige went back to watching her boys, wondering when they'd tire of the sun so she could justify going back to her cabin for a bit. Let them play with their Nintendo DSes or something while she had a pity party. "Nothing."

"Yes, you said something. I heard it, and you're wrong."

"No, I'm not," Paige said, turning to look at Daisy. Every other woman in the book club was in a relationship. Except her. Sure, Daisy didn't think she and Jared were a couple. *Sure they aren't.*

"It can be rather nauseating, am I right?" Daisy said with a laugh. "I mean, take Athena and Grey. They're so sugar sweet it's like they're dripping maple syrup or something. But they're about to get married, so they're allowed." She grinned. "Of course there's Tori and Chris, plus Ruby and Gabriel." Daisy nodded down the deck. "Even Ilana and Ethan are more lovey-dovey than I would have expected for how long they've been together. And don't get me started on Livvy and her sudden reawakening—the two of them really are acting like newlyweds. At least Shannon and her husband aren't syrupy." Daisy settled the baby on her lap and adjusted Sorrel's hat, even though they were in a shady spot.

Paige wasn't about to let Daisy's speech slide without taking the opportunity to include the last couple in their group. "And, of course, there's you and Jared."

"Wh-what?" Daisy pulled her sunglasses off and stared Paige down. "We *aren't* together. We *aren't* an item. And we most certainly are not ooey-gooey."

Right then Jared walked up and stopped at the foot of Daisy's deck chair. With the sun backlighting him, he almost glowed. Paige had to admit that he looked awfully good.

Excellent timing.

He held out a glass filled with pink liquid and a straw sticking out of it. "Thought you could use a raspberry daiquiri. No worries—it's virgin. I know you're still nursing."

Daisy took the glass in one hand and sipped from the straw. Her eyes rolled with pleasure, and she sighed. "That is delicious. Thanks."

Paige looked at Jared and tilted her head. "That was *so sweet* of you."

Daisy's eyes cut to Paige and threatened imminent death. Paige just smiled and blinked back innocently.

"Happy to help," Jared said, either unaware of the sudden tension or trying to ignore it. He clasped his hands. "Anything else? I thought Sorrel could use a nap and you could use a break. It's about time for his big-kid meal, isn't it?" He looked at his watch. "Quarter after two," he said, answering the question of what time it was, which Daisy had surely been about to ask.

"That—would be great," Daisy said.

Jared reached for little Sorrel and then, lifting him, Jared caught a whiff of the little guy's backside and made a face. "You are ripe, little guy. I think you need a change." He reached for the diaper bag beside Daisy, then gave her a little wink before heading out and waving Sorrel's hand in a mock farewell. "Bye, Mommy. See you soon."

When he was out of sight, Paige couldn't hold back her laughter. "What was that again about you two *not* being ooey-gooey?"

Daisy lowered her sunglasses and folded her arms. "We're *not* in a relationship."

"Methinks she doth protest too much," Paige said, enjoying the moment of teasing.

"I need a napkin," Daisy said, stood, and crossed the deck, presumably to the nearest bar.

Paige was tempted to call something out to her but held back. Maybe Daisy didn't realize what Jared was doing and hoping for, but everyone else with eyeballs did. Paige sighed, wishing she had a man pursuing her.

Her eyes trailed to her bag, where her phone sat. She'd managed to pay for a month's worth of international service so she could keep in touch with Derryl. It hadn't cost nearly as much as she'd feared. Thanks to the plan, her phone had dozens of texts they had exchanged over the course of the trip. Dozens over the last few days alone, if she was being honest with herself. She bit her lower lip and pondered the increase in his attentions. What did it mean?

He's not pursuing me. I don't think. I put an end to that. As I was supposed to.

Against her better judgment, she pulled out her phone and scrolled through the last few conversations she and Derryl had shared. The humor and kindness in his texts about the trip—asking how he could help her prepare, joking about hiding in a suitcase to come along—brought a melancholy smile to her face. She missed Derryl.

And not just since leaving for the cruise. She missed being with him. Being his girlfriend. He'd been a friend since their breakup in February, and she was grateful for that.

But she missed Derryl the boyfriend. Holding his hand as they took hours-long walks and talked. Hearing his ideas and opinions and having long conversations—something not conducive to texting. Watching Hitchcock movies with him as an excuse to snuggle close when she was scared—even if she wasn't. Kissing him under the light of the moon . . .

I gave all that up. It's not my right to ask for it anymore. I get texts and e-mails now, not moonlit walks on the beach and toe-curling kisses.

Her eyes strayed to her bag as she remembered some of the texts he'd sent since the cruise began. She pulled out her phone to read them.

Don't go letting some hot Greek guy sweep you off your feet.

She'd laughed at that one, but even so, her heart pattered a bit faster. Would he care so much if she did find someone else? The idea made her knees weak. The very last text she'd gotten was a little shorter.

Hope you're having a great trip!

Such simple words, but they went straight to her center, to the place where, deep inside, she knew the main reasons that had kept her from being in a serious relationship earlier in the year had gradually but oh-so-surely faded away, like the night before the dawn. Derryl still wasn't of her faith, yet he was such a *good* man. He was everything her ex wasn't, and he could bring so much happiness into her life and the lives of her boys now that she knew herself in a way she never had. She could stand on her own two feet and be strong without a man or anyone else propping her up—now she could, at least. She knew who Paige was. And she knew she could be the mom she wanted to be—and *had* been lately.

She'd reached many goals, and she'd come out of hard times stronger. If she found someone to date again, it could work this time. Not that there wouldn't be setbacks and problems, and yes, even hurt, but every relationship had those things, because human beings made mistakes. A relationship almost by definition meant setbacks and learning as well as the giddy, kissy moments Athena and Grey were experiencing right now.

Paige frowned and regrouped her thoughts. Time to watch the boys. Maybe herd them back to the cabin.

"Why the sad face?"

Paige looked up. Livvy stood there with a hand on one hip. "Hey," Paige said and forced a smile. "Where's your husband?"

"Taking a nap." Livvy laughed. "We hiked all over the ruins this morning. He's pretty wiped. Thought I'd catch some sun." She indicated a chair beside Paige—on the opposite side of where Daisy had been sitting.

"That's free," Paige said.

Livvy took the seat, but instead of stretching out in the sun and staying quiet, she clasped her hands, turned her knees toward Paige, and said, "So what's with the wrinkled forehead?"

"The what?"

With a motherly air, Livvy reached over and smoothed the worry lines from Paige's forehead. "There. Much better. Did you get bad news or something?" she asked, nodding toward Paige's cell phone.

"This? Oh no." Paige shook her head. "I'm just—" She cut off but then thought back to what Livvy had been through over the last year—how close she'd come to divorce but how much better her marriage was now. Paige's situation was totally different, but maybe . . .

"I need some advice." She hoped Daisy wouldn't return too soon. Paige knew exactly what *she* would say to this; she'd already made it perfectly clear that Paige was insane for breaking up with Derryl—a man who was rich and hot *and* had a great personality, as she put it.

"Shoot." Livvy sat up straight to listen.

"I'm still texting and e-mailing Derryl pretty regularly." She eyed Livvy for her reaction but couldn't read her expression. "I'm thinking it's not fair to him. But I don't want to stop."

"You broke up with him awhile ago, right?" Livvy asked as if reminding herself of the history. Paige nodded without saying more. "Hypothetically, if Derryl is still interested, would you still be interested?"

"Yeah. Maybe. I think so." Paige groaned. "I don't know."

"*Is* he still interested?"

"I think so," Paige said, hesitating. "But after all I've put him through, doesn't he deserve someone else? He'd probably figure I'm just stringing him along."

Livvy leaned forward, shaking her head. "Paige, Paige, Paige. Derryl deserves to be happy and with the woman he loves. If that's you, then he deserves *you*."

Paige looked at her phone again and then back at Livvy, a spark of hope igniting in her middle. She'd hurt Derryl; she knew that. Would reaching out be a slap in the face, or would he give the two of them another chance? He hadn't said a single word—not a hint—about getting back together in all the months since she'd called it off.

But today? What would happen if Derryl outright said he was still interested? Would she say yes? *I'd probably go running to him.* Paige felt her cheeks heat at the thought, but she kept herself from imagining what it would be like to be in his arms again, to kiss him again . . .

"I don't know," Paige said. "He's been so nice, but *nice* doesn't necessarily mean more than that. For all I know, he just could be helping out a single mom who needs it. He's a decent guy."

"Maybe," Olivia said with a nod. "Or maybe not. But you can't know if you don't reach out and tell him the door's open."

The idea, which had sounded divine a moment ago, now felt like a lead weight in Paige's stomach. "What if he says no? I don't know if I could handle losing his friendship too—and it could come to that. Even a man with the IQ of a snail wouldn't keep being friends with a woman who changed her mind every few months."

"Let me tell you something my mother used to tell me," Livvy said.

That's right—Livvy's mother and her "heaven reminders" were what Livvy lived her life by. And she'd done pretty well for herself. Paige swung her legs off the chair and leaned forward to listen.

"People think that to have a successful relationship, each person has to give 50 percent. Fifty-fifty, right?"

Paige began nodding until Livvy went on.

"Wrong." She lifted a finger in the air as if lecturing. "Each person has to give 100 percent. There will be times where you think that the other person isn't giving their full hundred, but you can't know that for sure. You're not in their head or heart, and you don't know how much effort they're giving. So you have to move forward, giving *your* hundred all the time." She sat back. "And that's what makes for a successful relationship."

Paige tried to process the whole conversation and apply it to herself and Derryl, when they didn't even *have* a relationship anymore. Or was it *yet*?

Yet. *I like the sound of that.*

"Derryl's already giving as much as he can," Paige said slowly, pondering. "I've set up some pretty strong boundaries, and he respects them. But he hints here and there that if I were to let him do more, he would."

The fact that he was still in contact with her at all was impressive, come to think of it. Livvy nodded her encouragement as Paige went on. "So for us to have any chance of success, *I* have to act next by letting him know that the boundary is moving—or even . . . gone?"

"Not quite, but almost," Livvy said, her eyes lighting up. "You have to do more than let him know the door isn't closed anymore. You have to open it up and walk right through it—do *your* 100 percent—so he knows where your heart is." She reached over and tapped Paige's phone, which had fallen off her lap onto the deck chair. "Let him know. And sooner than later, I'd say."

Daisy appeared then, less flustered than before and without her drink, which she must have finished on her own. "Sooner than later what?"

"I'd better get my boys inside," Paige said, but she knew her smile had to be betraying her. "Or they'll get burned to a crisp." She stood and gathered the boys' towels, the bottle of sunscreen, her bag, and, finally, her phone. "Boys," she called. "Time to get out of the water. I'll let you play DS for a *whole hour.*"

She never did that, but the bribe worked; Nate and Shawn barreled out of the water so fast Paige worried they'd slip. She toweled them off, then headed for the stairs.

She waved to Daisy and Livvy, mouthing, *Thanks*, before hurrying below deck with her boys.

Chapter 14
DAISY
SECOND CHANCES

IT WAS DAY FOUR—HALFWAY through the cruise—and Ruby had orchestrated a dinner for the entire group. It was wonderful to see everyone but perhaps a tad on the overwhelming side as Daisy tried to manage conversations and keep Sorrel happy at the end of what had been a long day for her little man. Jared graciously took turns with her, holding the baby so Daisy and he could eat for a few minutes at a time, but just three bites into the main course—curried shrimp—Sorrel lost all patience, and his temperament turned from unhappy to downright mad. Daisy stood and took him from Jared, bouncing a few steps back and forth to reduce the wail to a whimper, and then she looked out over the restaurant. Dozens of people had paid for the experience of this cruise, and Sorrel, for all his cute baby-ness, was ruining it for them. It didn't help that the sound of his cries made her breasts tingle as her milk let down. She was grateful he took a bottle so well, but for both their sakes, she needed to nurse at least every other feeding.

"I'm going to go," Daisy said after she made eye contact with Ruby, who rose to her feet as if about to offer to help with the baby. "Thank you so much for dinner."

Several people protested and offered to trade off with the baby, but Daisy had made her decision and graciously rejected each offer. "He's hungry and tired, and it's only going to be downhill from here." Embarrassed to be the center of attention, she smiled at Jared when he stood to help her get the diaper bag on her shoulder.

"I can take him so you can stay with your friends," he offered quietly enough that no one else could hear. However, his lowered tone created an intimacy that made Daisy aware of how many eyes were watching the two of them whispering together.

"It's okay. I'm pretty tired myself," Daisy said, still bouncing Sorrel, though he'd stuck his fist in his mouth and was only whimpering at the moment. She looked up into Jared's concerned face. "But thank you."

By the time they reached the cabin a few minutes later, Sorrel was wailing. Daisy turned the lights down to calm the mood a bit and then settled herself into the desk chair at the foot of her bed. She undid her blouse as quickly as possible and then let out a breath of relief when Sorrel latched on and went silent. Daisy's whole body relaxed with the familiar routine, and despite the chaos of the last few minutes, she sent a mental thank-you to both Paige and Olivia, who had convinced her to give breastfeeding a try for six weeks before she quit.

She'd remembered feeling rushed and anxious about nursing with her daughters, but she'd come to love the excuse to be still with her son, to focus on him and push away whatever else needed to be done at the moment. As a younger woman, she hadn't had the same perspective she had now, and she regretted not appreciating the opportunity to bond with her baby girls a little more. With this second chance—or third, really—she was doing things differently; better. She traced the side of Sorrel's face with her finger and smiled down at the amazing blessing he was in her life. Had there really been a time when she hadn't wanted this? It hadn't been that long ago, but the distance she felt from those thoughts was more than just time.

Daisy had to wake Sorrel up several times for him to finish eating. She didn't want him to realize three hours from now that he was hungry again. She put him down for the night in the crib provided by the cruise line and then sat on the chair again and picked up the book she'd bought at the airport. Since joining the book group, she'd come to enjoy reading more than she had for several years. She'd thought she'd be further into this particular book by this point on the cruise, but between the sightseeing and baby-bouncing and long talks with friends, she'd scarcely picked it up. She opened it to where she'd marked her place, but before she focused on the words of the story, she let the day wash over her.

In the port of Kusadasi they'd explored the city of Ephesus and seen the House of Virgin Mary in addition to checking out the shops near the port. Daisy had sent another postcard to her parents. It had been a wonderful day—perfect weather, beautiful views, and a cultural experience she'd remember forever.

What stood out more than any of those things, however, was Jared. Jared holding her hand as she stepped off the gangplank, Jared taking a picture of her, Stormy, and Sorrel with the sea behind them. Jared asking if she was tired, Jared bringing her a drink at the pool and then taking Sorrel back to his room for a nap. When she and Stormy had returned to the room an hour later, Daisy could hardly breathe as she'd looked at Jared, asleep on his side, with Sorrel curled into him.

Thinking about it now brought tears to her eyes, but she wasn't entirely sure why. Was it because of the bond Jared was forming with her son? Was it because of the gratitude she felt for Jared's amazing help since Sorrel's birth? Was it because Sorrel's own father had chosen not to be in their lives? It was all so confusing, and tender, and scary, and sweet. She tried to divert her attention back to the book, but after just a few sentences, she found herself thinking about when the cruise was over, when she and Jared returned to their usual schedules.

I'll miss having him so close, she admitted to herself. Rather than push away the emotion that came with the thought, she let it soak into her; she let herself feel every bit of it. She didn't fully understand what she was feeling toward her ex-husband right now, and she didn't dare wish for more than what the two of them had with one another, but she *would* miss him, and that anticipation made her sad. For a moment she considered trying to talk to him about her feelings, but as quickly as the thought came, she pushed it away. What did she have to offer him? What if sharing her thoughts created a barrier between them and she lost the friendship she'd come to cherish so much?

She heard tapping on the door, and expecting it to be Stormy telling her good night, Daisy put the book down and crossed the cabin. She opened the door quietly and painted on a wide grin to hide the thoughts she'd been entertaining. Rather than Stormy, Jared stood in the hall, filling the doorway and looking at her with a nervous smile.

"Oh, hi," Daisy said only a moment before realizing she hadn't finished buttoning up her shirt after feeding Sorrel. She pulled the sides of her shirt together at the neck, afraid that an apology would draw even more attention. She took a step into the hall and pulled the door mostly closed behind her.

"Hi," Jared said. He nodded past her toward the room. "How's the stowaway?"

"Sleeping like a baby," she said. Jared laughed at her pun, and she smiled wider. "He was fine once we got back to the room and he filled his belly. How was the rest of dinner?"

"Good," Jared said. "I like your friends."

"I'm glad."

They stared at one another for a few more beats, and Daisy had a sudden image of him taking her face in his hands and kissing her until she no longer remembered that they were divorced. The scene played out like a TV movie, and her mouth went dry.

"I wondered if you wanted to go for a walk on deck with me and watch the sun set."

There was no justification in his request that had anything to do with Stormy and Sorrel, or even Shannon and John, whom they'd had a nice evening with a couple of nights ago. It was just Jared wanting to spend time with *her*. She automatically tried to come up with a reason to say no. She couldn't cross this line. She wasn't ready. Out loud, however, her heart betrayed her.

"I'd love to, but Sorrel is asleep."

"Stormy said she'd be here to watch him in just a—" A door closed with a snap farther down the hall, and Jared looked that direction. "Here she is."

A moment later, Stormy joined them outside the room. "Where's he at?" she said as she stepped past Daisy and pushed the door open.

"He's asleep," Daisy whispered, following her inside.

She pointed out the diapers and bottles, and Stormy kept saying, "I know," over and over until Daisy closed her mouth and took a breath.

"Thanks," Daisy said.

"No problem," Stormy said, waving off her mother's gratitude and picking up the remote for the TV. "And don't worry. I'll keep the sound low."

Daisy nodded, then turned toward Jared, who leaned against the doorframe with his hands in his pockets and a soft smile as he watched them. The dim light of the room and backlight from the hallway emphasized the breadth of his shoulders and shadow of his jawline to the point where Daisy had to force herself to look away.

"You ready?" Jared asked, sending a shiver down her spine.

Daisy just nodded, then glanced in the mirror and leaned forward to fluff her hair. She wished she could change into something a bit more slimming.

"Don't you kids stay out too late," Stormy said as she sat on the bed and scrolled through the TV stations. "If you're not back by curfew, I'm taking the keys to your car and your phones, and you can't go out with your little friends tomorrow night."

Daisy and Jared both laughed, and Daisy stepped past him into the hallway. He pulled the door shut and nodded toward the forward section of the ship. "Have you been to deck 7?"

"No," Daisy said, shaking her head.

"It's the spa deck, so it's busy during the day but pretty empty in the evenings. The views are amazing."

They took the elevator to the seventh floor, then went through the automatic doors onto the deck, which wrapped around the ship. A few other people were out there smoking or reading or snuggling; Daisy tried not to look at them too closely. The deck narrowed, and Jared fell a step behind but kept his hand on the small of her back as they continued forward. After a few yards, the deck opened to an area with small tables and some lounge chairs.

Other than a couple who sat on the far side, the deck was empty. Jared stepped ahead of her to the front railing. Daisy reached it a step behind him and looked out on the ocean reflecting the golden light of the setting sun. The view *was* breathtaking—just as Jared had promised—but the view wasn't the only reason Daisy was having a hard time taking a full breath right now. She was so aware of him, so distracted by his nearness and his invitation to come up here in the first place. Her mind raced while her heart seemed to beat in spite of a kind of giddiness growing within her chest.

"Are you going to raise your arms and yell, 'I'm king of the world'?" she asked in an attempt to distract herself from her confusing thoughts and emotions.

Jared laughed and leaned his forearms on the railing. "Being king of the world sounds like a lot of work," he said, turning his head to look at her. "At my age, I'm interested in taking things a bit easier."

"*Your* age," Daisy said, nudging him with her shoulder as she too rested her forearms on the rail. "You're younger than I am."

"By seven months, two weeks, and—"

"Four days," they said at the same time. They held each other's eyes for a moment and then both looked forward and let a comfortable silence fall between them.

"It's so beautiful here," Daisy said as she looked at the shoreline in the distance and the setting sun to the west. The violet-blue water stretching out before them was mesmerizing but not enough to distract her from how close she and Jared were to each other.

"It is beautiful," Jared said, but she sensed him looking at her and felt her neck heat up in response to the implication. Surely she was reading too much in the comment, right? She willed herself to continue facing forward but heard him move and peeked sideways. He'd turned so his hip was leaning against the railing, and he'd crossed his arms over his chest. For the first time she sensed a heaviness about him, as though he was pulling together the resolve to do something difficult.

"Jared?" she asked. "Are you okay?"

He didn't look at her for a few moments, but when he did, there was a vulnerability about his expression that caused Daisy to imagine that whatever she said right at this moment would burrow into him somehow and forever become part of who he was. It was a startling thought—rather poetic and romantic for Daisy to have thought of at all.

"Do you think people change, Daisy?" Jared finally asked. The wind blew his hair, but he didn't take his eyes off her, and she worried that he was seeing the same vulnerability in her face she'd seen in his moments earlier.

"I think people *can* change, but they don't always do it."

Jared accepted the answer with a nod and turned to face the sea again. "What makes the difference, do you think? What makes someone change or not change?"

This was a deeper conversation than Daisy was used to having with anyone, let alone her ex-husband. For years their conversations had been limited to topics relating to Stormy, though in the last several months things had certainly changed between them. Daisy felt an expectant energy about this conversation; where would it take them?

"I don't think anything *makes* people change," Daisy said. "I think people are changed through their responses to what happens to them. They're changed through what they decide they want out of life—goals and things like that—and how they work toward them."

Jared looked at her with a thoughtful expression. "So, people change when they choose to change as a result of something that happens to them or in hopes of something they want to happen?"

"Sort of." Daisy didn't feel as confident in her answer, so she tried to better organize her thoughts. "I think everyone is faced with challenges. *Crossroads* may be a better word. They can choose what direction they take at certain junctions. Those choices and a person's commitment to them and the things learned along the way can change a person's character. Maybe I'm not making sense."

"No, you're making sense," Jared said. "So for instance, a woman ready to be done with motherhood finds herself pregnant and faces a crossroads as to how she responds to the change."

Daisy felt her face heating up and quickly looked down at the bow of the ship cutting through the water. "I didn't know we were talking about me," she said, reviewing her comment. Yes, she'd been faced with an unexpected crossroads when she had learned she was pregnant, and she had made the decision to take on the responsibility of raising another child. That had been an important choice, one that had definitely changed her, but raising Sorrel was a far cry from anything heroic—especially when she thought about how hard the decision had been and how many uncomfortable realizations about herself it had forced her to face.

"We're talking about everyone, and anyone, *and* you, and me," Jared clarified. "But that situation would be a good example, wouldn't it?"

"I suppose." Daisy gripped the railing with both hands and leaned back in an attempt to look casual, though she feared it looked anything but. "I don't think I'm a different person, though. Just wiser. Better. More mature, I guess."

"What about a man who wasn't a very good husband? Do you think he could change?"

"If he chooses to, yes," she said, immediately thinking about Sorrel's biological father, Paul, who was now Daisy's most recent ex-husband. "Are we talking about anyone in particular?"

Paul had faced the same crossroads she had with an unexpected pregnancy but had made a very different choice. Though their marriage had been good, it had been based on his very specific expectations, not on the level of commitment that an unplanned future had suddenly presented them. She certainly was not over the grief of their marriage failing, but the divorce was easier to understand once she'd realized Paul hadn't been the caliber of man she'd thought he was in the beginning. Sooner or later *something* would have happened to show her that. The fact that the something was another person—the human life they'd created—only made his true colors show that much more boldly. She felt duped into having thought she'd known him and could at least appreciate the fact that Paul revoking his parental rights meant he would have no influence on her son, whom she fully expected to grow into a good and responsible man.

"We're talking about me," Jared said, drawing Daisy back to the question she'd asked him regarding whether they were talking about anyone in particular.

She felt her eyebrows rise in surprise as Jared watched her reaction. "Oh," she said lamely, then thought about his question in regard to *himself.* Could a bad husband change his ways?

Why was he asking her that?

"Do you think I've changed since our divorce?" Jared asked.

"You don't think you were a good husband?" she asked, then an instant later remembered how things had ended and hurried to add, "Let's not count the last year."

"We can't be fair without it," Jared said.

She sensed shame in his voice; it softened her feelings about that time even more. She'd acknowledged forgiveness to herself but not to him. "Well, if it's about fairness, we have to be completely fair about the three years before that last one."

She took a breath and said a little prayer for strength to say the next words the right way. "First, we moved way too fast in our relationship, and I got pregnant before either of us knew each other as well as we should have—we hadn't even talked about marriage. You had plenty of reasons not to marry me—we were both unprepared—but you didn't turn your back on us. You not only took on the responsibility of husband, but you became a father to December, the daughter I already had, and after Stormy was born, you were an excellent dad to her too. You put your personal aspirations for acting on the back burner and got a steady job to support us. You took a second job so I could work part-time after Stormy was born, and when I got pregnant again—after things had already fallen apart—you were willing to do the right thing all over again, even though we weren't happy together anymore. We both hoped a baby would heal us. After I miscarried—"

"I cheated on you and—"

"Remember, we're leaving out the last year," Daisy reminded him, though hearing him say the words so bluntly stung.

He went quiet, and they both stood there, the words settling around them like dead autumn leaves—brown and brittle. Daisy turned to look at him, and the wind blew her hair in front of her face. With one hand, she gathered it into a ponytail, holding it so she could look at him staring at the water, lost in memories she wished they could ignore. She put her free hand over his hand that was gripping the rail and gave it a squeeze.

"Jared," she said softly. He looked up at her, and she opened her mouth to explain her feelings, but he cut her off before she'd said a single word.

"I'm so sorry, Daisy," he said quietly. "I'm so very sorry for what I did."

"I know," Daisy said.

"But I've never said it."

"And I'm glad to hear it now," Daisy said. "But I've forgiven you—forgiven us."

"Us?" He shook his head. "You don't have responsibility for what I did."

"No, I don't," Daisy said. "But I do have responsibility for the fact that our marriage wasn't based on the kind of solid friendship it should have been. When I found out I was pregnant with Stormy, I begged you to marry me and make it legitimate. I'm not saying it was the wrong decision, but it was entirely selfish on my part. I don't know if we'd have ever married if not for Stormy, but I wanted you to validate me and help me satisfy my parents' expectations. I wanted you to give that to me, yet I was thinking very little about *you* at all. I didn't think about what you wanted, or what you had to give up, or how I could make sure our marriage was more than a family for Stormy. I put little effort into our relationship, and when you gave me a good excuse to get out, I didn't hesitate. *That* responsibility belongs to me."

"To both of us," Jared said.

"Maybe," Daisy said. "But I don't regret having married you, and I don't blame you for the fact that it didn't work. Please don't try to carry the failure of our marriage on your shoulders."

"But if—"

"Truly," Daisy said, giving him a pointed look. "I don't want to talk about how it ended. I'm at peace with our past and am so grateful we've made it work with Stormy, not to mention the amazing support you've been to me with Sorrel. I don't know how I could have done it without you these last months."

Jared's pinched forehead made him look doubtful. He didn't look away from her, and the resulting heat flushing her body as he stared at her reminded her that her hand was still covering his. She quickly removed it and placed it on the rail again.

"I have loved being a part of your and Sorrel's life." He stared at their hands side by side on the white railing. "But I'm struggling to understand *us*. What are we to each other now?"

"I don't know," Daisy whispered. His eyes came back to meet hers, and she could feel her heart picking up speed. She felt him touch her and watched as he put his hand over hers. Daisy spread her hand, allowing his fingers to fit within the spaces.

"Would you say we're friends?" Jared asked.

Daisy looked into his face—his searching and vulnerable face—and nodded.

"Would you say we're more than that?" he pressed.

Daisy didn't know how to answer. They *were* friends, and every interaction they'd had these last months reflected that—he'd helped her with details of her life she struggled to manage, and she'd cooked him dinner, picked up his dry cleaning when she was running errands, and expressed her gratitude continually. She'd had *thoughts* that went beyond friendship—especially on this trip—but they had been equal parts excitement and confusion.

She thought hard about her answer before she spoke, weighing the risks against the potential. "I don't know how to define what we've become, but I'm open to the idea of being more than friends." Saying it out loud made her feel exposed in front of him, raw and revealed and wishing she could take back the words. All of the complications she'd thought about—the baggage they both carried—avalanched toward her, and she felt her face flame as she looked away from his eyes and chided herself for being so agonizingly honest. She let go of her hair and grasped the railing to steady herself, refusing to look at him or their hands, which were still joined. More than friends; what would he say to that?

"Really?" The optimism in Jared's voice stopped her spiraling fears. She looked up at him amid her hair dancing around her face. He wasn't smiling, exactly, but he looked enthusiastic. "You'd consider having us . . . date?"

Daisy couldn't help but smile at the boyish excitement of his question. The term *date* sounded so juvenile. They were nearing their fifties, for heaven's sake, and they had an eighteen-year-old daughter.

"Dating sounds so . . . young and carefree," she admitted. "I just got divorced, I have a new baby, and . . . I'm not sure I can trust my own motivations." She reflected on what her motivations to date Jared could be. To avoid the loneliness she often felt in the evenings when Sorrel was asleep and the apartment was too quiet? The idea of Sorrel growing up in a family instead of as the son of a single mom? Or maybe it was because she felt better when she was with Jared than she ever felt without him. She felt taken care of and supported—but admitting that to herself raised even more questions. Was she feeling dependent on him? Was she being selfish again to want to be with him for her own reasons?

"Seeing you with Sorrel has been one of the most beautiful things I've ever witnessed," Jared said.

She met his eyes, then looked away, embarrassed by the unfiltered admiration she saw there. Admiration she didn't deserve but took pride in all the same. "If there's a hero in this story, it's you, Jared."

"Not hardly," Jared said, shaking his head. "*My* motivations *are* entirely selfish." He pulled their still-joined hands from the rail but didn't let go of her.

"How so?" Daisy said, feeling breathless.

"Having Stormy move back in with me has been great," he began. "I had forgotten what it felt like to be a dad morning to night, and while I know she's more adult than child these days, I've loved getting closer to her. Watching everything that happened with Paul and the way you pushed through it was amazing, and then to see you being a mother again—to see the softness and kindness I think sometimes you forget is there—has reminded me of all the good times we had together. I understand what you said about not having the foundation of friendship we needed to make our marriage work, but we still enjoyed each other; we still brought out the best in each other, at least some of the time."

Flashes of their life together slid through Daisy's memory—a sailing trip to Catalina, family time at the beach, a hundred surprise tulips coming up in the spring after Jared had planted them without her knowing it in the fall. Other moments—intimate ones—reminded her of the chemistry they'd had as well. Jared had always been affectionate, quick to kiss her on the cheek or pull her to him when they watched TV. He'd once told her she was the most beautiful woman he'd ever met, and she'd believed it.

"There *were* a lot of wonderful times, weren't there?" she said.

Jared reached out and brushed some hair out of her face, then took a step forward, forcing her to look up to maintain eye contact. An excited thrill ran through her at his nearness. "I would like to date you again, Daisy. I would like to see if we can't build the foundation we were missing the first time—something strong and good and wonderful. We know each other's histories, strengths, and weaknesses, and while I know we both bring a lot with us, maybe it's not *all* bad. I think I'm more Jared than I was before, and you're more Daisy than you could have been back then.

I think we better understand ourselves now, and because of that we can better understand how to make each other happy."

She wanted to ask him detailed questions, like *Are you sure you don't mind having Sorrel in the middle of this? What if we fail? What if things get ugly?* Yet as she looked into those beautiful blue eyes and felt the anticipation build of just how good they could be together, she realized that the answers would reveal themselves. They would need to talk to Stormy about it and make sure she understood. Yet they were already divorced, and they'd already raised their daughter separate from each other, and Stormy was an adult herself now. Just as Daisy had committed to be a better mother this time around, couldn't she be a better partner, too?

"And I don't want to rush things," Jared added before Daisy could formulate a response. "I want us to be absolutely certain with each step we take that we're ready. It will mean doing things differently than last time— talking differently, acting differently, planning differently."

That was exactly what she needed to hear. She needed to know they'd be wise in how they moved forward, that they'd continually evaluate their momentum and think of all the people involved in the choices they made. But beyond it all, she realized with every part of her that she *wanted* this second chance. In a way completely impossible for her to articulate, this felt *right*. She nodded, afraid that if she tried to explain she would make a mess of it.

Jared slid his hand from hers and put it on her waist, causing her whole body to shiver. "So, we're doing this?" he asked, that youthful excitement in his tone again. "We're going to be a couple and see where it goes?"

Daisy had to laugh at the beautiful sweetness of his words. "Yes," she said in a breathy whisper as the wind whipped her hair into a frenzy and Jared smiled down at her.

He tilted his head slightly, enough to remind Daisy of the thousands of times she'd seen that movement—the silent invitation, the moving in but not completing the approach. He was waiting for her to fill the blank space between them. It had been nearly fifteen years since she'd kissed this man, but in an instant she relived every one of those kisses, remembered every thrilling second of them, and yet she knew that *this* kiss—the one they would share for a mere moment—would perhaps be the most unforgettable of them all. She raised up on her toes, lifting her head while holding his eyes, which deepened and darkened in response to her willingness. His hand on her waist slid around her back and pulled her softly against him. His other hand brushed her hair from her face. "To second chances," he said, lowering his mouth to hers. Their lips met, and the last of Daisy's reservations melted away as she was reminded of the fact that the very best things in her life had always been the most unexpected.

Chapter 15
ATHENA
WEDDING BELLS

"You look gorgeous," Jackie said, standing back from Athena and smiling.

Athena couldn't help the tears that started to form, ones that would surely streak her mascara, but then she remembered she was wearing waterproof—because Jackie had thought of everything.

Athena gazed at the women surrounding her in the church dressing room: Jackie, Ruby, and Olivia. Looking at them just made her want to cry more. Olivia turned out to be a whiz seamstress when she repaired a small tear in the wedding dress. The gown was of the softest ivory silk Athena had ever touched, and it hung off her shoulders, coming to a V in the back. The unadorned bodice flowed to the ground. It had no train, fancy lace or beadwork, just simple elegance. And it couldn't have been more perfect.

Ruby pulled out a velvet box from her clutch. "These are for you, dear."

Athena opened the box to see a beautiful set of pearl earrings and a necklace. The women gasped, and Athena brought a hand to her mouth at the sight.

"Ruby," Athena said in a reverent voice. "They're beautiful. You are too generous." Her eyes smarted.

"You deserve the best on your wedding day," Ruby said, her voice trembling with emotion. She lifted the strand of pearls, and Jackie helped fasten them around Athena's neck.

"I feel like royalty," Athena said, touching the smooth pearls. She put on the earrings and turned to the full-length, gilded mirror. Amazing how a wedding dress could transform her. And it helped that she stood in a beautiful church just outside of Athens.

A year ago Athena had been content with her uncommitted life, avoiding her mother's antics of setting her up with blind dates, stringing Karl along . . . That had all changed when she'd met Grey.

Jackie reached for Athena's hand, and Athena grasped Jackie's. Even though her parents couldn't be here, she had Jackie and her book-club friends who had become so dear to her, not to mention several cousins, aunts, and uncles from Greece waiting outside for her.

"Ready?" Jackie asked.

Athena nodded even though her stomach was knotting up. As if on cue, music struck up inside the chapel, vibrating through the stone walls. The solemn chords seemed to travel to her core, filling and steadying her. She was nervous, but she also couldn't wait to see Grey at the end of the aisle.

Athena turned to Ruby and hugged her gently, then moved to Olivia for another hug. Finally, she embraced Jackie. "Thank you," she whispered, her voice catching.

Jackie drew away, tears glistening. "I'm so happy for you."

Athena opened the dressing-room door, and she smiled at Gabriel standing outside, waiting to escort her down the aisle. With his tuxedo and dazzling grin, he looked like a posh movie star. Athena heard a small gasp of appreciation from Ruby. He held out his arm, and Athena grasped it, grateful for his presence.

He leaned down and kissed her cheek. "You look stunning."

Athena could only smile because she didn't think she could speak without crumbling with emotion. She caught the wink Gabriel threw Ruby's direction and imagined Ruby's flushed but pleased face. It was good to know a man could have such a sweet effect on Ruby.

They walked along the narrow stone corridor toward the chapel. Huge arrangements of flowers stood on each side of the entrance, and a garland followed the stone archway. Jackie's daughters, Maria and Eleni, waited by the closed wooden doors, looking adorable in pale pink dresses and holding miniature bouquets.

Next to the girls, a priest stood waiting to open the doors.

"Ready?" Gabriel asked.

Athena nodded, her heart drumming inside her.

The priest opened the doors with a smile, allowing the two girls to enter first. Maria and Eleni started down the aisle, and the audience turned their heads toward them.

Athena's breath hitched as she saw the people she loved. It was an incredible sight, and she was glad they'd decided to have the ceremony in her parents' homeland. So many faces she loved, including the book-club ladies and others she'd be getting to know better, such as Grey's brother, Jed. The chapel was lovely, with stained-glass windows, stone architecture, and flowers filling every spare space.

The smiling faces blended together, and the music seemed to fade as she looked down the aisle. At the end, Grey faced her, wearing a dark-gray tuxedo, hands clasped in front of him.

Seeing Grey shouldn't have surprised her, but it did, sending a jolt through her heart. Grey was really standing in a chapel, next to a priest, surrounded by flowers and wedding guests . . . waiting for *her* to walk down the aisle and marry him!

She felt overwhelmed as her emotions collided—love, gratitude, awe. She would have melted into a puddle if Gabriel hadn't been there to hold her up. Somehow she managed to take one step, then another, and before she knew it she was practically floating toward Grey.

In part of her mind, she knew the tears were back, but she didn't care. She saw only Grey. She wanted to run into his arms and kiss him, but that would have to wait. Grey's smile widened as she drew closer, and he reached for her hands as soon as Gabriel let go.

As Grey's warm hands enclosed hers, she gazed into his eyes—feeling the love in them travel to her heart.

"Hi," he whispered.

"Hi," she whispered back.

He held her gaze, his eyes intent on hers, and she felt as if she were about to dissolve on the spot. The priest began his speech. Athena squeezed Grey's hands, if only to stay upright and to focus on what the priest was saying. It was part Greek, part English, and Athena let the words wash over her, filling all the holes of emptiness her parents' absence had created.

"I love you," Grey mouthed, his fingers threading through hers, somehow making it feel like they were the only two inside the church.

Then Athena realized the priest had gone quiet.

"Yes, I do," Grey said.

Our vows.

She looked at the priest, then back to Grey as the priest asked if she'd take Grey as her husband. She inhaled, letting the scented air fill her. "Yes, I do."

The rest was a blur as they exchanged rings and the priest pronounced them man and wife. Then Grey pulled her into his arms and smiled down at her. She clung to him as he kissed her until they were practically pried apart by their guests. Athena embraced everyone in turn as Grey stayed at her side, keeping one of her hands firmly in his.

When they moved outside, the sun was just beginning to set, casting a rose-hued web of light across the gardens. A band played some soft music as the guests seated themselves. Athena and Grey walked past the decorated tables to the head table, which was covered with a lace tablecloth.

"Come on," Grey said. "Let's dance first."

Athena glanced at the guests taking their places. "Are you sure?"

Grey looked at her and smiled, then leaned down and whispered, "It's our wedding, and I want to dance with my wife." He signaled the waiters, indicating that they should start serving the guests. Turning back to Athena, he said, "We can eat later."

His warm breath on her ear sent a shiver through her body. "All right, Mr. Ronning. If you insist."

His arm encircled her waist, and he guided her to an open space in front of the band. She wrapped her arms around his neck, and he pulled her close, swaying to the music.

"I'm so glad you showed up to the wedding," she said.

"Are you kidding?" He drew away slightly, his eyes settling on her. "Nothing could have kept me away."

"That's good to hear," she whispered, moving closer.

"Did I tell you that you look beautiful?" he asked, his voice lowering.

"Not today." Athena touched the pearls at her neckline. "Ruby gave these to me."

"They're perfect with your dress . . ." His hands moved to her hips, his gaze soaking her in. "Which is beautiful too, by the way."

"It's better than what I was wearing when we first met—all sweaty in my jogging clothes."

He laughed, then pulled her against him. "I love all of your looks, Athena."

"Mmm," she said, melting into his scent. "And I love all of you."

Other couples started dancing near them, and Athena decided waiting to eat was definitely a good choice. There was nowhere she'd rather be than right here, in Grey's arms. She closed her eyes, just breathing him in and feeling his heart beat against her. He turned his face and whispered, "You know you're mine now, don't you?"

She smiled. "And you're mine."

"Maybe we can slip out and go back to the ship," he said. "Do you think anyone would mind?"

Athena laughed. "I wouldn't, but I have about a dozen cousins who would."

"Good point," Grey said, and she could hear the smile in his voice. "Let's get it over with. We'll eat, take a few pictures, cut the cake, and then we'll be free."

"Why are you in such a hurry?" Athena asked in teasing voice, pulling away slightly. The look he gave her made her blush. "Be patient."

"I've been *very* patient," he said, then leaned down and kissed her.

People around them cheered, making Athena blush even more, but that didn't stop Grey from kissing her long and hard. When he pulled back, she almost wished they didn't have to go through the formalities of the wedding celebration.

Next to them, Tori and Christopher were clapping. Athena laughed, feeling a little embarrassed. Tori wore a classy white dress, though it was a bit odd to wear white to someone else's wedding. Maybe it was a Hollywood fad.

Christopher gave Grey a hearty handshake and a clap on the back. Then Athena noticed Daisy and Jared standing there—together. Had they been dancing too? Before she could speculate, Paige came over and gave her a hug.

She looked radiant in a turquoise gown that matched the blue of her eyes. For a second, Athena wished Paige had a date at the wedding. "You look great," Athena said.

"Thanks, and you're gorgeous," Paige said. "I'm so happy for you."

The other ladies soon surrounded Athena, congratulating her.

Grey's hand found hers again, and a few moments later they made their way to the head table. Grey's arm stayed around her shoulders until their food was served. Then the toasts began, one after the other.

Athena's Greek family wasn't shy about taking turns. Each of her cousins stood to say something. They gave touching tributes, mostly about missing her parents and how grateful they were to be together as a family. Athena wiped away tears more than once, but she knew she was in for it when Ruby stood.

"Dear Athena and Grey," Ruby said, holding up a glass of champagne. "The love you two have is as priceless as a flawless diamond. Always treasure it. Never let it fade. Don't forget to do the little things for each other. And always be willing to forgive each other." She paused, her voice trembling. "If I were to give one bit of advice, it would be to never think you're alone. You have each other, and the more you give, the more you'll receive."

Everyone clapped, and Grey wrapped his arm around Athena's shoulders. She nestled against him and wished the magic could go on forever. But soon they'd return to the States, and everyone would get back to their own lives. Athena decided to cherish this moment here and now. Things weren't perfect—her mother never got to see her married, and her father's mind would never be clear enough to understand who Grey was—but she had a thousand other things to be grateful for.

Athena watched Gabriel and Ruby dancing and laughing together. Paige was cutting up meat for her two adorable boys—ever the attentive mother—while visiting with Athena's uncle and aunt. Daisy and Jared looked pretty cozy sitting next to each other, Sorrel sound asleep against Jared's shoulder. Stormy was flirting with a couple of Athena's younger cousins; apparently there wasn't much of a language barrier tonight.

Victoria and Christopher had disappeared somewhere, and Ilana and Ethan were slowly walking around the perimeter of the party, hand in hand. Shannon and John walked near them, John's arm around his wife, in some sort of conversation with Ilana and her husband. And dear Olivia and Nick were dancing, their eyes closed, as if they were in their own world.

"Happy?" Grey whispered in her ear.

She turned to see his smiling eyes. "More than happy. Thanks for finding me, Grey."

"I think you found me," he said. "You showed up at my bookstore, remember?"

She smiled, her heart full. "Then thanks for not letting me go."

Chapter 16

VICTORIA
OUR OWN TERMS

TORI'S HEART POUNDED SO HARD in her chest she worried a rib or two might break. Chris had her hand tight in his as he led her away from Athena's wedding. She wanted to look back at her friends and Athena's happy moment but didn't want to draw anyone's attention, so she didn't turn around. If only they could all be present for what she was about to do. But it was chancy enough to have Ilana, Ethan, Shannon, and John in on her secret. The fewer people who knew, the better.

The sounds of their feet as they descended the stone steps echoed through her thoughts. "Are we doing the right thing?" she whispered, finally voicing her doubts. Her parents would miss her wedding. Her dad wouldn't be there to give her away. The things she'd always wanted . . .

But this had almost been her mom's idea from the beginning. Tori knew the families would all understand.

Chris stopped on the stairs where they were low enough to no longer be seen by anyone from Athena's wedding. There were a *lot* of stairs leading to this particular church. He took both of her hands in his and cradled them to his chest. "What did your mom say to you before we left on the cruise?"

Tori held his gaze even though her vision blurred over the pain of her mom not being there with her. "That if we came back a married couple, she wouldn't blame us, and she'd be proud we chose to live under our own terms."

"*Our own terms*, writer lady. So, yes, I think we're doing the right thing. But if you don't feel good about it, if these are just my terms and not yours, we can back out now. We don't have to do this."

He meant it. She knew he did. Even after all the planning and preparing he'd done to make sure the paperwork was right, to arrange the time and location for it to take place right after Athena's wedding. He'd drop everything if it was what she wanted.

But none of their options were what she *really* wanted. She wanted a private wedding that included her parents, his parents, and their friends. One that *didn't* include the media snapping pictures to combine with cruel and misleading captions. One that *didn't* include crazy people putting packages with bombs in them among the presents. This chance with Chris tonight was the closest she'd get to what she really wanted. Because marrying Chris *was* what she really wanted.

She looked into his eyes—so full of love and hope for their future, so full of understanding if she chose differently from their prearranged plans. "No. You're right. This is our only chance. Besides, what is more romantic than a secret wedding to the love of my life?" She tugged him into a brief, determined kiss. When she pulled away, she tightened her grip on his hand and looked down to the sea glowing in the fiery sunset. They continued their descent and wound their way along the path at the bottom until they began climbing again to a different church.

They'd had to use a Protestant church to get the documentation in order. Chris originally wanted to do a seaside wedding, but that would have required them to be in Athens for weeks prior to the wedding to sign paperwork at city hall. Besides, Tori's mom would be glad they were married in a church.

Shannon and Ilana would follow after them. She'd asked them to stagger their exits so as not to raise suspicion. She was glad these two women would be there with her and hated leaving the others out, but between needing to keep things secret and not wanting to take away from Athena's wedding, this was best.

The pastor was waiting at the top of the stairs just outside the wooden doors of the church. He smiled when he saw them. "I was worried," he said in a thick accent.

Chris smiled and shook the priest's hand. "Just coming from another wedding is all."

"You'll have witnesses?" the pastor asked.

"Yes," Tori answered. "They should be here any minute now." She turned to look behind her as if she expected Shannon and Ilana to be standing there and blinked in surprise at what she saw instead.

Ruby and Gabriel were a ways down the stairs but were rapidly approaching. Chris squeezed Tori's hand. When she looked at him, she saw a flicker of amusement cross his features.

"Ruby! Gabriel! What are you guys doing here?" she asked when they were finally close enough.

Ruby lifted her eyebrows. "I saw you sneaking off. The better question is what are *you* doing here?"

Gabriel wore a knowing smirk.

Tori took a deep breath, trying to find the words to explain, but Chris beat her to it. "We're getting married. You can both keep a secret, right? Care to join us?"

Just like that.

Chris was definitely not a beat-around-the-bush kind of guy. She smiled gratefully at him.

At first, Ruby seemed struck speechless by the news, but then she clapped her hands in excitement. "Join you? Of course I want to join you," Ruby said. "But why would you plan all this and not invite me in the first place?" She sounded hurt.

Tori released Chris's hand for the first time since they'd left Athena's wedding. She wrapped her arms around Ruby's neck and felt tears burn behind her eyelids. "I wanted to. I wanted to invite all of you, but that's so many people to be in on a really big secret."

"But this is *me* we're talking about." Ruby shook her head and pulled back from Tori's embrace to look her in the eye. "I was the one who knew you were engaged before you told your own mother. I didn't tell anyone, not even Gabriel, and I tell him everything!"

Gabriel smiled and took in a breath that puffed out his chest a little. He apparently liked hearing that he was her confidant.

"I know," Tori said. "And believe me, I wanted to invite you right from the first, but the closest thing Athena has to a mom is *you*. I couldn't take that away from her on the most important day of her life. I wanted to make sure you could be there for her completely. It's bad enough I wore white to someone else's wedding and that I'm basically hijacking her day by stealing away Shannon and Ilana."

As if on cue, the two women showed up with their husbands. Shannon shot Ruby a look of surprise, then shot another look at Tori, which seemed to be probing for information on how Tori felt over Ruby's sudden appearance. "Aunt Ruby! Hi. Everything okay?"

"Of course it is," Ruby said, wrapping her shawl over her shoulders. "I'm just here to see another woman I love like a daughter get married. Wouldn't miss it for anything." She smiled and took Gabriel's hand.

Tori smiled too and gave Ruby another hug, not caring that Ruby's hand was attached to Gabriel's. "I'm glad you're here. If I can't have my own mom, there isn't anyone else who could better fill that role."

Ethan tapped the case he carried over his shoulder. "I've got my camera so we can film the whole thing in top quality so your parents can watch it later. It's the next best thing to being there."

Chris clapped Ethan on the shoulder. "You're one in a million. I appreciate you thinking ahead."

Ilana smiled at her husband.

Chris held his arm out to Tori. "So . . . Victoria Winters, how about we change that name of yours?"

She took his arm, and together they led the way into the church. The inside looked similar to the place they'd just left, with its stained-glass windows and arched doorway leading to the chapel. Chris had obviously done his research and worked hard to find a beautiful place. Ethan pulled out his camera and took some footage of the surroundings—another thing Tori appreciated. She didn't want to forget one detail of this magical night, and she was sure her parents would want to see as much of her wedding as possible. She felt certain Chris wanted the same for his parents.

She started to walk up the aisle with Chris, but he stopped her. "This isn't a Vegas wedding, writer-lady. We're doing this old school." He linked her arm to Gabriel's. "If you'd do the honors of giving this woman away, I'd be grateful."

"As long as I give her to you, right?" Gabriel said with a grin.

"Give her to anyone else and I'll press charges for kidnapping."

Everyone laughed at the banter. Chris went over to the pastor, who was in a corner untying the ribbon off a box.

Tori flinched at the thought of the bomb threat, then felt foolish. No one knew about this wedding. Of course there wouldn't be a bomb in that package, but the tightening in her chest eased considerably when instead of something explosive Chris pulled out a bouquet filled with white calla lilies and orchids. He presented the bouquet to Tori with tenderness in his eyes, making her heart swell with love. He really had thought of everything.

They were doing this. They were really going to be married. And then no one—no contract, no sense of company loyalty, no rabid, lunatic fan could take that away from them. As she looked into his eyes, she found there was nowhere else she wanted to be and no one else she wanted to have by her side.

He ran the back of his fingers against her cheek. "Ready?"

She nodded. "To marry you? I've been ready since I first laid eyes on you." She smiled. "This is going to sound strange, but I wish Max were here."

"I know."

"Do you think he'll understand? It feels like we're letting him down somehow."

"Max will still get his Hollywood wedding. You once told me Max was your friend, and I believe he is. I believe he's a good man. He'd have to be to gain your loyalty. And we'll have a zillion bomb-sniffing dogs at that Hollywood event. But I don't want bomb-sniffing dogs and fear in my bride's heart on the day we truly give ourselves to each other. I want my bride feeling happy and safe. This is the only way to get that. As your friend, Max would want your happiness. He'd want this for you."

Tori nodded again. Chris was right. Max *was* her friend. He would want her happiness. As she allowed her gaze to slide over her surroundings, she found she was happy. And she felt safer than she'd felt in a long time.

Chris kissed her cheek and leaned in close to whisper, "I'll collect a real kiss at the other end of this aisle."

Gabriel cleared his throat to stifle a chuckle.

Chris strode purposefully to the end of the aisle. The little group took their places at the front, all except Ethan, who stayed back to make certain he could get adequate coverage, and Ruby, who lingered an extra moment at the back of the church with Tori. "You're a beautiful bride, Victoria Winters." Ruby gave Tori a quick hug before taking her place next to Shannon.

Tori squared her shoulders. Christopher Caine could have chosen any of those bachelorette beauties. But he'd chosen her. She was at her own secret wedding about to marry the man who read books just so he could discuss them with her, the man who made her heart skip beats.

The pastor cued his organist, and music filled the chapel. Tori took her first step toward the future she had once believed impossible.

She only vaguely remembered the priest, the words he spoke, and the words she and Chris exchanged. When Chris was invited to kiss his bride, he made good on his promise of a real kiss at the end of the aisle. All her insides felt melty and fiery, right down to her toes. People laughed when Chris dipped her back, apparently having no intention of ending that kiss.

Tori finally broke away with her own laugh. "We're in a church," she whispered. "It's not the place to be obscene."

"Says the girl who helps organize kisses for a nationwide viewing audience," he whispered back.

"Not *this* kiss." She dropped her bouquet to the ground and kissed him again, relishing the warmth and safety he represented.

She felt Chris smile against her lips as he said, "Definitely not *that* kiss."

They joined hands and turned to their small gathering of friends. There were no movie cameras to smile for, no scripted dialogue. She hugged her friends, starting with Ruby, who had been there from the beginning. She smiled and laughed because she *wanted* to smile and laugh, not because the nationwide audience expected it from her. Chris took Tori's hand, and with their fingers laced together they left the church.

And instead of flashbulbs from the paparazzi, the gorgeous velvet night sky of Athens greeted them with a million stars that seemed to shine in celebration of the start of their lives together.

The one we'll live on our own terms.

Chapter 17

ILANA
AT LAST

WHEN THE CRUISE SHIP DOCKED in Sicily the day after Athena's wedding, Ilana and Ethan took the opportunity to go ashore. The island was far too large to cover in the time they had left, so they had to decide what to do—visit ruins or eat at a restaurant or take a walk along the beach. They settled on meandering through some ruins; Ilana had forgotten the name because she'd been distracted by other thoughts, but she enjoyed the rustic architecture, the blue, blue sky, and the smell of salt in the air.

They walked hand in hand on stones people long dead had walked upon, past columns and half-disintegrated walls. Ilana couldn't help but wonder about those who had once lived here, what being a woman in this city would have been like thousands of years ago. She imagined a boy hiding behind one of those columns and watching a girl help her mother pick out the best olives at the market. The ruins spoke to her as if the ghosts of the past were whispering that their legacy wasn't their columns or buildings or theater—no, their legacy was their families and the lives they spent loving and caring for each other.

She squeezed Ethan's hand, feeling her love for him swell inside her. He squeezed back and smiled down at her as they walked. How had she gotten so lucky to be with such a good man, one who stood by her side through thick and thin—especially with how *thin* their life had become thanks to all she'd put him through this last year? Yet through everything, he'd never once blamed her or accused her; he'd just loved her and believed in her more than she had believed in herself.

Neither said much as they walked, although Ethan sometimes consulted a pamphlet about the ruins and read information about what they were looking at. He also stopped by every placard to read the information aloud, a quirk she loved about him. The information he read was interesting, and under other circumstances she would have soaked it all in, but right now she had other things on her mind, things she needed to tell him but didn't know how.

Ilana could hardly believe it, but throughout the cruise, something had slowly worked inside her, making a dramatic change in her mind and heart.

Maybe it was the magic of spending a week on the water, of seeing Greece and Italy. She had to admit that pulling into the port at Messina had looked like something out of a Kenneth Branagh movie. Or perhaps it was the romance of seeing Athena and Tori both find their happily ever afters. Or watching Paige and Daisy up close as they interacted with their children—and witnessing the genuine joy and love the two women had with and for their kids.

Whatever it was, something had shifted and settled in her heart as if a key had turned, sending a tumbler moving into its rightful place, opening her up to new possibilities—and to the future she was meant to have, leaving her heart wide open. She thought again of the papers she'd filled out, which she'd taken out of her purse and put in her suitcase beneath a pair of jeans so Ethan wouldn't come across them before she was ready.

But now it was time he knew.

Ethan led her over to a set of ancient stairs, where they sat and looked out over the landscape, the shore, and the almost unbelievable blues of the sea, which went from turquoise at the coast to dark sapphire as the ocean deepened. It was breathtaking. Ilana closed her eyes and inhaled the fresh air, leaning against her husband as he settled an arm around her shoulders. This was better than any buzz she'd ever gotten from pain pills. This was true happiness. She reached one hand into her jeans pocket to feel the outline of her ninety-day chip.

Soon to be replaced by my 120-day chip. Back when she'd first gotten her white one-day chip, which marked twenty-four hours sober, it had felt like a monumental accomplishment. At the time, she'd doubted her ability to earn any chips marking longer periods of sobriety.

But now . . . now she didn't doubt or wonder or speculate. She *knew* she'd reach 120 days, and eventually she'd start counting her sobriety in years. It wasn't that the temptation to take pills was somehow gone, vanished in a cloud of magician's smoke. No, she was an addict and always would be. But she now had the means to cope with her emotions, to find ways to manage other than by medicating herself into a stupor instead of facing problems head on. Those skills were her new superpower in fighting the cravings and the urge for a buzz that felt good in the moment but would only sabotage her life—and her sweet husband's life—in the long run. Nothing was worth that.

If I were in a drug haze, I wouldn't be able to enjoy this view—or Ethan—right now.

He alone was reason to stay clean. So was the child—children?—out there waiting for the two of them to be their parents.

Do it, she told herself. *Tell him.*

Ilana cleared her throat and dove in, glad she could look out on the ocean rather than stare at his face when she felt so vulnerable. "So . . . I've been thinking . . ."

"Mmm?" Ethan tilted his head so it rested over hers, then leaned in to kiss her temple as he often did.

She breathed deeply with a contentment that gave her the courage to continue. "I've been doing more than thinking, actually."

"About what?" Ethan's voice was casual and curious, as if she'd been pondering what kind of Italian food she wanted to find for their dinner rather than something with the potential to change their lives completely.

"Well . . ." Another breath. *Here goes.* "I've been doing some research on costs and what paperwork would be involved, and I talked to a lawyer . . ."

Ethan stiffened beside her. "A lawyer?" His voice sounded tense.

Realizing with a start that he probably thought she meant a divorce lawyer, Ilana straightened and turned to him. "Oh no. Nothing like that. I'm happy—happier than I've been in years." She reached up and cradled his face between her hands, then leaned in and kissed him as further proof. "Really."

He looked at her warily but nodded. "Okay . . . so what does a lawyer have to do with anything?" His eyes narrowed. "What exactly have you been researching?"

She swallowed and soldiered on. "I've been researching China. And Vietnam. Africa may be the best bet, though, and quicker, if one website I looked at is accurate."

Ethan's face registered hope. Ilana could tell he wanted her to be talking about adoption.

But he cleared his throat, and when he spoke, his tone was wary. "Are you, um, thinking about another vacation or something?"

Ilana bit her lip with excited anticipation as her pulse quickened. Ethan had wanted to adopt for so long but had backed off these last several months after she'd told him she was in no place to even *think* about it. But she wasn't entirely sure what *he'd* think of an international adoption—a child of a different race and background.

"Ethan, I want to adopt a baby. I'm ready to take that step." She clamped her mouth shut, clasped her hands tightly, and waited for his reaction.

A series of emotions crossed Ethan's face—confusion, wonder, excitement, and then wariness again. "You—wait. I mean . . . What?"

"I want us to have a family. I'm finally ready."

Ethan held her by the shoulders and gazed at her, concern etched around his eyes. "Are you sure? No doing this for me. It's still so soon after your . . ." His voice trailed off, but she knew he meant either her hysterectomy or her rehab—possibly both.

"It is fast—I know that." She looked around them and shrugged. "But you know that all I've ever wanted is to be a mother."

"But you said—"

Ilana shook her head and put a finger to her husband's lips. "I know. I wasn't ready then. But I am now. Before this trip, I did the research and talked to the lawyer and even got the paperwork for adopting a little boy from Africa or a girl from China—I wasn't about to make a final decision without consulting you, but I felt like I needed to explore it on my own—without any pressure—to make sure the process didn't scare me away." She smiled at that, realizing how far she'd gone without getting scared away. "Granted, when we got on the ship and I saw Paige and Daisy, I freaked out. They looked like old pros, like they'd been born knowing how to care for a child. I didn't have the slightest clue what to do with a baby or a toddler. I almost ripped the papers up and threw them overboard."

A smile finally stretched across Ethan's face, and his eyes looked glassy, as if they held unshed tears of joy. "What changed?" he asked, searching her face.

She shook her head, her mind tumbling with thoughts and the memories of the gamut of emotions she'd felt in recent days and weeks. "Everything has changed. I want to move on to the next chapter of our lives. I'd regret sitting around for the rest of my life, refusing to be a mother just because we couldn't pass along our DNA. I can do this.

I'm even more sure after this trip, watching Daisy care for her son after thinking she couldn't do it again, and Paige—she never expected to be a single mother, but she glows around her boys, and she has friends to help her. So do I." She bit her lower lip and smiled. "I'm ready. I *want* to do this."

Ethan's unshed tears now began to trickle down his cheeks. With the back of his hand, he wiped them away, then reached over and tucked a strand of Ilana's eternally curly hair behind one ear. "You never cease to amaze me, Ilana Goldstein."

She searched his eyes. "So that's a yes? You want to do it?"

"It's an absolute, positive yes." He pulled her close in a tight embrace and then kissed her, soft and long, until her toes curled in her sneakers. He pulled back and rested his forehead against hers. Her lips tingled with his kiss in a way they hadn't for a long time.

A lot has changed . . . for the better.

"So," Ethan said, fingering her hair. "Are the initial papers ready to go? I understand it's a lengthy process."

She nodded. "This first set just needs our signatures. We'd have to find a notary. And an international adoption will cost an awful lot. It can take years—"

Ethan's gaze softened into one filled with emotions from joy and relief to unfulfilled longing. "I'd pay a fortune and wait a lifetime if it means we get to be parents."

She leaned in and kissed him again. "At last."

Chapter 18
VICTORIA
DISCOVERED

WHEN TORI AND CHRIS HAD booked their cruise, they'd reserved two adjoining rooms so they wouldn't have to explain anything to the rest of the book group when they were finally married and officially celebrating a honeymoon. The fewer people who knew, the better.

Still, they each went separately to retire for the night and took circuitous routes to their rooms so they appeared to be alone. They didn't want to leave any wiggle room for conjecture or lucky guesses—especially after seeing the tabloid in Greece. If the Grecians had magazines with the couple's faces on the cover, they were not as incognito as they'd first hoped. No one could know about this wedding. The studio would have her flayed and left to dry in the sun if they discovered Tori had breached yet another contract.

Taking the long way the first time wasn't that hard, since, in her nervousness over her first night as a married woman she'd ended up on the wrong deck. Chris had a good laugh when he found out what had taken her so long.

They were equally cautious anytime they left their rooms, never leaving or returning at the same time. They thought they'd gotten away with their latest contract breach, but when they awoke to fervent pounding on the door the next day, Tori flew out of bed, confused by the knocking. Was all that noise happening on her room door or his? Who was supposed to answer it? She threw a robe on and stared at the door in confusion.

Chris apparently woke with greater mental lucidity because he shooed her to her side of the adjoining rooms and shut her out. She tried to listen while he answered the knock.

She pressed her ear tightly to the door, straining to hear and understand the frantic voice. She nearly toppled to the floor when the door whipped open to reveal Chris standing in a T-shirt and boxers and . . .

"Ruby?" Tori shot a questioning look toward Chris. "What are you doing here this early?" It wasn't early; it was the middle of the afternoon, but in newly married terms it might as well have been two in the morning.

Ruby held a rolled-up newspaper. She unfurled it so Tori and Chris could see the picture taking up nearly the entire front page of the entertainment section.

Tori covered her mouth.

The picture was after their wedding at the moment they had exited the church hand in hand to start their lives. And while it was a decent picture, the fact that it existed at all, in a *newspaper*, was really *bad*.

"How?" Tori asked when she was sure she could speak without throwing up or screaming.

Chris began pacing. "Someone from the ship had to have recognized us. Or maybe somebody from Athens. They must have followed us. There isn't another explanation."

"Are you going to be in trouble?" Ruby asked.

Tori nodded, still feeling sluggish in spite of her pounding heart and knotted stomach. They were in enormous trouble. The studio would be furious. They'd yank her movie deal from preproduction.

And there would be a lawsuit . . .

Tori groaned and finally sat on the bed on Chris's side to keep from passing out. She had to call Max. Tell him before he found out on his own. She owed him that much. Max might have been a ruthless director, but he was also one of her dearest friends. She couldn't let him find out by way of tabloid that she'd stabbed him in the back—again.

She grabbed for her phone, but Chris, anticipating her move, got to it before she did. "Let's think this through before you tangle yourself into a situation that might be otherwise fixable."

She couldn't believe he'd used that word. "How is anything *fixable*?"

He sat next to her, putting an arm around her shoulders. "Have some faith." He turned to Ruby. "Could you please go find Ethan? We need all of the footage he took of the wedding."

Ruby rushed out to obey Chris's request.

Chris got up, changed into jeans, and threw a Hawaiian shirt over his T-shirt, leaving it unbuttoned. She watched, wishing she understood what he was hoping to accomplish. "What are you doing?" she finally asked.

He took a moment to sit back next to her and cradle both of her hands in his. "Think, writer-lady. How did we get out of trouble when we broke the first set of contracts?"

"Robert pitched an alternative . . . Oh . . ." She smiled, thinking of the cameraman who had been one of her best friends since she'd started working on *Vows*. She felt a sliver of hope take root in her heart. "You mean . . . *we* could pitch an alternative film."

"Right. Ethan filmed the whole wedding for us. He was awesome about it. He shot it from all angles; he's also taken several shots of us on the cruise and at various ports. Robert will be happy about all of that. What if we get one of the studio guys to mix all that footage into something awesome and then give the studio the exclusive rights to our secret wedding? The very fact that it *was* a secret wedding is a huge selling point. Sure, some idiot got a picture of us on our way out, but the very fact that the photo is of us outside the church means they didn't get anything inside. Plus, that photo is kind of grainy. Max and Darren would be fools to pass up the opportunity. What's better? None of the set dressing, food, or wardrobe changes have to be paid for by the studio. We've saved them a fortune!"

"That could work . . ." Tori's thoughts raced ahead to all the implications and ways the plan could backfire, but all she could think was that they really had a chance for this to be okay.

Chris kissed her forehead. "Of course it will work. It's all about how you sell it, and Mrs. Caine? You married an expert salesman."

"Really?" Tori allowed herself to smile. "Expert, huh?"

He shrugged. "You don't sell half the world its peanut butter without a good marketing plan." He moved to his feet again and opened the door to leave. "Get dressed. I'll be back in a *tick*, as your neighbor says."

"Where are you going?" Tori asked.

"To get some information."

Tori shook her head to show she didn't understand.

"Can't run a marketing campaign without a little market research." He checked his pocket for his phone and shut the door.

She sat on the bed a moment longer before jumping to her feet. He was right. She needed to get dressed and ready for the day, prepared for whatever happened next. No matter what, she wouldn't apologize for her actions. She would never apologize for saying "I do" to the man she loved, even with the worry of unhinged fans taking potshots in the crowd.

But she would do whatever she could to make it as painless as possible for the studio. She owed that to Max and her producer, Darren. She owed them her very best efforts to give them what they needed, and she couldn't do that running around in a robe.

By the time Tori had showered and dressed, Ruby had returned, saying she couldn't find Ethan or Ilana, likely because they'd done a shore excursion in Sicily. Ruby had left a message for them to be in contact as soon as they returned. Ruby offered hugs and moral support before leaving again.

Tori got on the phone, glad she'd switched to the international calling options with her service provider. She dialed Robert's number and begged the universe that wherever he was, it wasn't anywhere near Max or Darren.

He answered. "Hey, Tor, what's up? I thought you were on vacation."

"I am. But I have a bit of a problem and really, really need some help."

She explained the situation in detail, starting with the bomb threat and all the subsequent choices. To his credit, Robert didn't sigh or give any lectures. He simply listened.

"Tell me *somebody* filmed it," he said.

"My friend's husband did."

"Did he use a crap camera? Or worse? Tell me he didn't use his cell phone."

She looked out the windows to the balcony and wondered what was taking Chris so long. He'd love to know how well he'd predicted Robert's reaction. "He's a doctor with a good income and buys decent equipment. No ghetto cameras. He even used a tripod for some of it."

Only then did Robert sigh in relief. "Bring me the footage as soon as you hit California soil. And I want every picture from that trip."

"Chris is collecting the footage now."

"Love that our most rogue bachelor is also our smartest bachelor."

"What if he and I both wrote a journal of sorts from each of our points of view? We could do some voice-overs . . ."

"I like that. Definitely do that. We'll record the voice-overs as soon as you get back. But Tori, *you* have to tell Max. You can't sit on this for another minute. So far I haven't seen any press, but that doesn't mean Max hasn't."

Robert was right. She told him as much, thanked him profusely for remaining her truest friend, and waited for Chris to come back. She wanted to call Max after gaining all available information.

Chris returned carrying Ethan's camera.

"How did you get that?" she asked. "Ruby said they were doing a shore visit."

"You don't even want to know," he said with a wink. "But it's amazing how much being nice to all the stewards this whole time pays off. Oh, and I called my lawyer. He went over the contracts with me and thinks that as long as we provide them with exclusive footage from our wedding, we've fulfilled our obligations contractually. I researched and watched all the *Vows* wedding ceremonies months ago to get ready for the show. Our wedding is a million times more authentic and romantic than anything Max ever directed."

"True enough, but Max does do an amazing job, and so does Robert," Tori said. "And . . . I need to call Max."

Chris looked doubtful. "You sure you don't want to wait until we have things cinched up tight first? We should watch some of this footage together so we know what we're really offering."

She agreed. Eyes wide open usually worked best. Chris connected the camera to his laptop, and they sat close together on the bed to watch. Tori wiped at her eyes and felt a little guilty to be grinning when they had once again landed in a huge contractual disaster, but . . . "Our wedding was pretty amazing, wasn't it?"

He gave a soft smile. "How could it not be when it involved the world's most beautiful woman?"

"This will work," she said before they'd finished watching everything. "I need to call Max now." Tori told Chris about her call to Robert and the voice-over idea and how they could use all of the stills they'd taken of the cruise during the voice-over recording. "It's not just about wriggling our way out of the contract. It's about me being a good friend and helping Max save face at the studio."

Chris nodded his agreement. He didn't totally love Max, but he knew Tori did, and he supported that friendship.

Tori took a deep breath and dialed the number. It was a long conversation filled with a little yelling, a little tension, a few long moments of silence, a little "Why didn't you call me first?" and a lot of something unexpected—Max understood. And he actually liked the idea of having access to a secret film. He said it fit perfectly with the insanity of the rest of the season. Viewers liked to be kept on their toes.

Max reminded her that there would be no financial compensation for the film. Tori and Chris both agreed that was totally fine.

"I wish I could've been there, kid," Max said.

Tori's breath hitched in her throat. "I wish you could have been there too."

"But I get it. I won't say I'm thrilled, and I really wished you would have trusted me to protect you, but I get it. Tell that peanut farmer congratulations for getting the best girl I know."

"I will."

"And Tori?"

"Yeah?"

"Love you, kid."

She smiled and met Chris's gaze. "I love you too, Max."

She hung up, still smiling, her eyes tearing up for reasons she couldn't really explain. "I guess that's it, then. Max has declared us free and clear. We're officially done with being the bachelor and bachelorette."

Chris took her in his arms. "Good, because I think *husband and wife* is so much better."

She snuggled into his arms, breathing in the scent of him, and couldn't help but agree. Being husband and wife was *definitely* better.

Chapter 19

RUBY
YES

RUBY HADN'T STOPPED CRYING SINCE Athena and Grey's wedding—at least it seemed that way. Watching Paige with her sweet kids made her teary eyed, seeing Daisy and Jared smile at each other made her heart swell, and knowing that Tori and Christopher had secretly married away from all the media made her want to giggle madly, especially now that the crisis over their wedding being discovered had been averted.

As she leaned against the rail of her balcony watching the sunset fill the sky with gorgeous pink and peach, her heart was full. She felt a bit wistful thinking of the challenges that continued with Keisha—but now that Shannon and John were a united front, they'd be strong together. The cruise had been a wonderful break for them, and Ruby had never seen Shannon so friendly with the book-club ladies. True friendships had developed.

Ruby smiled as she thought about the light she'd seen in Ilana's eyes on the cruise, and she chuckled, remembering Livvy and her husband acting like two high schoolers with crushes on each other. Everywhere she turned, everyone she interacted with was happy. Love seemed ever present when the group was together—in hugs, smiles, laughs, and conversations. She and Gabriel had spent a magical day ashore in Sicily, browsing the markets and touring several sights. Ruby's favorite sight had been Toarmina's Porta Cantina, where they spent time at the gorgeous plaza that offered an extraordinary panoramic view of the gulf. They had lunch at a historical café on the Piazza and visited the gothic churches. They didn't see everything—they'd been in no hurry—but simply spent time together, hand in hand.

Dinner was in twenty minutes, and Ruby would again be surrounded by some of the dearest people in the world to her. Amazing that only a year ago she'd delivered fliers to start the book club, dropping one off at a Barnes and Noble, where she met Daisy, and leaving one at Grey's Used Books, which led to meeting Athena. The other women had called when they'd spotted one of her fliers. And now these ladies had become so important to her. What a magical year, and all of it culminating in a cruise together. She couldn't believe that tonight was the final evening of the cruise.

Ruby's heart soared as she thought about her friends and how close they'd become to her. She wanted nothing more than to see them happy and healthy, and she knew they wanted her happiness in return. Athena, despite her newlywed-induced haze, had not let up in her comments about Ruby and Gabriel being the next bride and groom.

Of course Ruby had laughed them off, knowing Athena couldn't really guess that Gabriel had already given Ruby a ring, which was tucked safely in her room's safe. She'd taken it out several times to look at it, then quickly put it back inside. It was a beautiful piece of jewelry, and it echoed Gabriel's thoughtfulness. He always thought things through—sometimes too much so about his ex-wife—but Ruby wouldn't have him any other way.

She turned from the balcony and the fiery orange of the sky and looked over her tidy stateroom. Although she'd have plenty of time to pack tomorrow, she'd done most of it already, leaving out only what she'd wear to bed tonight, her toiletries, and a change of clothing for the morning. Her gaze landed on her new purse—the one Gabriel had haggled for in Crete.

Little had Ruby known that when Gabriel was buying that purse he had already planned to give her the ring in just a couple hours' time. She let out a soft sigh, thinking of him. Every moment she wasn't with Gabriel she missed him, and she couldn't imagine not having him in her life now. But marriage was . . . so involved. A blending of families. What would her son, Tony, think about having a stepdad?

The thought made her heart race, and she turned back to look over the gently moving ocean. It would be strange to see her son and Gabriel together. And when Tony and his wife, Kara, would finally decide to give her a grandchild, they'd be grandparents. Ruby brought a hand to her mouth. *If* she and Gabriel married, they'd be grandparents. She closed her eyes, breathing in the warm ocean air. Would marriage to him be so difficult?

Gabriel loved her; she loved him.

He would be true to her—she knew that much without a doubt, even in the dark places of her heart, places Gabriel had brought light to.

With a sigh, she walked into her room, closed the balcony door, and grabbed her new purse. It held all of the essentials she couldn't part with and some she carried in case someone else needed them. She touched up her lipstick in the tiny bathroom mirror and smoothed her pale green blouse. Her green-and-silver earrings had been purchased in Sicily earlier that day. Another gift from Gabriel.

She slipped on her strappy silver sandals, a great find at the Fashion Island mall before the cruise. Ready now, she left the room and stepped into the hallway. Coming down the corridor were Athena and Grey, arms around each other, with Athena leaning her head on Grey's shoulder as they slowly walked. Ruby's heart tugged at seeing the two together, so content after having gone through so much. They were finally together, married, and moving forward in their lives.

"On your way to dinner?" Athena said with a smile when she spotted Ruby.

"Yes, dear," Ruby said. "Can you believe it's the last night of the cruise?"

"It's hard to believe," Grey said, squeezing Athena's shoulder.

"Yeah, it's been incredible." Athena stopped in front of Ruby and leaned in for a hug. "You look great. And I love the purse. That Gabriel is a keeper."

Normally, Ruby would have laughed, but for some reason her eyes filled with tears.

"Are you okay?" Athena asked, furrowing her brow.

Ruby dabbed at the renegade tears. "Don't mind me. I've been a bit weepy. Probably my age or something." She tried to smile but couldn't.

"I'll catch up with you, Grey," Athena said in a quiet voice.

Before Ruby could protest by telling the couple to continue without her, Grey had leaned down, kissed Athena's cheek, and gone ahead of them.

"Really, I'm fine," she told Athena.

Athena leaned against the wall and folded her arms, a knowing look on her face as she waited for Ruby to spill it.

Ruby exhaled. "All right. I need to . . ." Her voice started to tremble. "Show you something." She unlocked her door and led the way inside her room. She crossed to the far wall and opened the safe. Inside lay the ring box.

Athens stared at it. "Is that . . . ?"

"Yes." Ruby's eyes filled with tears again. She opened the box, and Athena gasped.

"It's gorgeous." Athena took the ring from the tiny velvet cushion. She held it up to the light coming from the balcony. "It's perfect for you. I mean—" She cut herself off and looked at Ruby.

"It *is* perfect," Ruby said, sniffling.

"Then why are you crying?" Athena asked, her own eyes watering. "I don't even know why *I'm* crying. Shouldn't this be wonderful news? What did you tell him? . . . What did you say?"

"He didn't ask for an answer," Ruby said, taking a deep, shuddering breath. She told Athena about the walk to the St. Mary's church in Crete and how Gabriel had knelt down but had said it wasn't a proposal. "He told me that when I was ready to become Mrs. Alexakis . . . to wear this ring."

"Oh." Athena's eyes went wide. "Oh." Her gaze went back to the ring. "So you are keeping it in the safe until you . . . decide?"

"Yes," Ruby whispered. "But . . ." Tears coursed down her cheeks now. "I'm tired of sending him home at night. I'm tired of being alone."

Athena wiped her own eyes and smiled. "Then wear the ring."

"It's not that simple." Ruby's heart felt heavy, and her head hurt. The emotions now coursing through her left her feeling exhausted.

"It *is* that simple," Athena said in a quiet voice. She lifted Ruby's hand and pressed the ring into her palm, then closed her fingers over it. "You had no problem telling me to marry Grey."

"Because you're perfect for each other; anyone can see that," Ruby said.

Athena's smile was soft. "*I* didn't, not for a long time. In fact, I broke up with him."

Ruby chuckled despite the tears. "You did. You were very stubborn."

Athena raised her brows, watching Ruby.

"What? You're saying *I'm* stubborn?" Ruby opened her hand and looked at the ring, then back at Athena. "This isn't about being stubborn. I was married for thirty years. But you—not every woman is lucky enough to find someone like Grey."

"Or . . . Gabriel," Athena said, placing her hand on Ruby's arm. "It's time to stop living in the past. Make new memories. If anyone knows how scary stepping into a new relationship is, I do."

Ruby blinked against the burning in her eyes as she stared at the ring in her hand. Her throat was too tight to speak. Athena squeezed her arm. A few moments later, when Ruby looked up, she realized that Athena had left the room. Now it was just Ruby and a ring with a diamond surrounded by rubies.

She closed her eyes for a moment and focused her thoughts on Gabriel. *How does he make me feel? Loved. How do I feel about him? I love him.* She opened her eyes as a breathless excitement pulsed through her.

She slipped the ring on her finger.

Then she left the room without checking her makeup. If her face was blotchy from tears, so be it. Her smile would make up for that.

The corridors were empty as she walked to the dining room. She would be the last one there. She hoped Gabriel had saved her a place next to him. Of course he would have; it wasn't even a question.

When she entered, she greeted the hostess, who immediately knew which table to lead her to. Everyone was already seated, laughing and talking, their plates piled with food.

A smile tugged at Ruby's mouth, but inside her heart was pounding. Athena faced Ruby as she walked in, and when she looked up, her gaze went to Ruby's hand.

Ruby felt a rush of heat go through her as Athena spotted the ring and gave her a small smile. Ruby could tell she was holding back. But there was no turning around now. Athena had seen it. She knew.

Ruby continued forward and glanced around the table. She saw Gabriel's profile as he talked to Jared. An empty seat sat right next to Gabriel. Of course. The men laughed at something. Ruby stopped and watched Gabriel, her heart overflowing. This sweet man was everything to her.

She took another step forward and then another. Gabriel turned and saw her. He had dressed up like the other men in a button-down shirt and tie. His dark hair was combed back, but its natural wave had rebelled a bit. His olive skin looked golden in the soft light of the restaurant. Standing, Gabriel pulled out her chair as his brown eyes soaked her in.

"I was about to come find you," he said, leaning down to kiss her cheek. "You look beautiful."

"Thank you," Ruby said, grasping his hand and squeezing. His gaze went to their hands, just as she'd hoped.

He touched the ring, then his finger traced the gems. "Ruby?" His voice was a husky whisper.

She couldn't answer because her throat had suddenly swelled. She looked up at him, blinking back tears. She tried to smile, but that didn't work either.

His hands moved to her waist, and he pulled her tightly against him. Ruby melted into his embrace, so warm, so strong, so Gabriel. Then he kissed her. Right there in front of all of their friends. And Ruby didn't care.

It took only seconds for everyone else to catch on, and pretty soon they were clapping and cheering. Ruby pulled away, laughing and crying at the same time.

Gabriel cradled her face with both of his hands. "You don't know what this means to me." He gave her a light kiss on the lips, then lifted her hand and kissed her ring finger.

Soon they were surrounded by the others, hugging and backslapping, and swept away by the congratulations. Ruby finally reached Athena and pulled her into a tight hug.

When Athena released her, her eyes were wet with tears. "You deserve every happiness, Ruby. Thank you for one of the best memories ever."

Chapter 20
ATHENA
Newlywed

DESPITE BEING UP LATE THE previous night for the final dinner of the cruise and not being able to fall asleep for a while after that—which she fully blamed on her new husband—Athena was awake early. Once she'd gotten used to the time change, her body clock had gone back to its early-morning schedule.

And now that she'd been married thirty-six hours, it seemed her mind was craving routine once again, although the break had been divine. She looked over at Grey, who was dead asleep next to her. He lay on his stomach and had one arm flung across her torso as if he couldn't sleep without touching her.

The thought made Athena smile.

The last few days—the entire cruise, really—had been surreal. Perfect. But she knew that lurking outside of this wedding trip was a lot of work on the magazine. She surely had dozens of e-mails to address and the other half of the next issue's layout to do.

Jackie had been staying in touch with their dad by calling the care center and checking up on him. It was strange being so far away from him. If anything happened, Athena wouldn't know about it immediately, and she was too far away to help. She exhaled. Everything had been lovely, but the wedding was over, and she felt the pressure mounting.

Sliding from beneath Grey's arm, she climbed out of bed and changed into some clothes. If she could just spent thirty minutes in the business center on her e-mail she'd be able to enjoy the final breakfast with the book-club ladies, then prepare to spend the day in Rome before the red-eye flight across the Atlantic.

It was 5:30 a.m. If she hurried, she'd be able to fit everything in. She sat on the edge of the bed to pull on her shoes, and a hand snaked around her waist.

Athena yelped as Grey dragged her down and pinned her beneath him.

"Where are you going?" His voice was scratchy, but his gaze was intent.

"The . . . weight room?" she said, hiding a smile.

He lifted an eyebrow as if he didn't believe her. Of course he knew better.

"I mean . . ." she said. "The business center. But only for a few minutes. Promise."

"Can it wait?" He lowered his head and kissed her neck.

"I won't be long."

"Mmm," he mumbled, his lips now kissing her jawline.

"I'll be back before you know it," she said, closing her eyes as heat traveled through her body at Grey's touch.

"Stay here," he said, his mouth capturing hers as he pulled her down.

Athena wrapped her arms about his neck, kissing him back. The weight of his body against hers pretty much changed her mind.

Grey lifted his head. "E-mail?"

It took her a moment to focus. "It hasn't been coming through on my phone."

He brushed a finger along her forehead, then kissed her again. "I'll come with you."

Now she was surprised. "You have work to do?"

"My job is to dote on you." He grinned, then rolled off her. Standing next to the bed, he held out a hand. "My wife owns a major travel magazine, and I'm not going to hold her back."

Athena grasped his hand and let him pull her up from the bed. His hands encircled her waist. "Besides, I'll want your full attention when you're done."

It was almost a sin how sweet he was. She looked forward to thanking him properly. He let go of her and pulled on his shorts and then a T-shirt. "Come on," he said, grasping her hand. "Let's get hot chocolate on the way."

Once in the business center, Grey was true to his word. After making Athena the most perfect cup of hot chocolate, he jumped on another computer to go through his own e-mails. The place was deserted, so there was no rush to finish quickly. Grey wrapped up before her, and after that, he fiddled with his phone, taking subversive peeks in her direction. Sometimes he'd go so far as to lean in for a small kiss.

Finally, Athena couldn't stand it any longer. She logged out of the computer, then rose from her chair and sat on Grey's lap, wrapping her arms around his neck. "You're too much," she said with a laugh.

"Better than being too little." He smirked and pulled her close.

"Don't change," she whispered.

"I won't if you won't," he said, brushing a kiss on her cheek.

"Deal."

His mouth found hers, and as Athena melted into the all-encompassing kiss, she couldn't believe she'd ever broken up with this man. And now she was Mrs. Ronning.

"Are you finished?" he eventually asked.

She kissed him once more before answering, "Yes."

"We should probably go back to our room," he said, his breath warm on her skin. "I don't think we want someone walking in on us."

Athena blushed and stood. By the time they made it back to their room, she was laughing at herself for getting so distracted.

Once back at their room, Grey helped her put together thank-you gifts for the book-club ladies, which she'd present to them at breakfast. It had been hard to come up with the perfect thing, but she'd picked out small crystal statues of the Parthenon. Grey wrapped them in tissue paper while Athena wrote the thank-you cards.

When they finished, Athena hugged Grey good-bye and made her way to the banquet room she'd reserved for the breakfast so there could be more privacy. Ruby was already there, talking to Paige. Athena set down the gift bags and hugged both women.

She grasped Ruby's hand, admiring the ring. "Still wearing it?"

Ruby laughed. "I think Gabriel would prefer to glue it to my finger."

"I don't think he has to worry," Paige said with a smile.

"Where are your boys?" Athena asked Paige.

"Jackie offered to watch them." She shrugged. "I guess this will almost be like a real book-club meeting."

Athena nodded, but her heart tugged a little for Paige. All of the other women had come on the cruise with their significant other, and Daisy and Jared seemed to be rebuilding their relationship. Paige was the only one left without a husband or boyfriend. But judging by the brightness of Paige's eyes and her healthy complexion, she'd loved the cruise.

"I'm so glad we were all on the cruise together," Athena said.

Ilana and Daisy came walking into the lounge. Daisy didn't have her baby. Either Jared or Stormy must be watching him. Athena hugged both women, realizing she was becoming a mini Ruby as she went around hugging people, but she was too happy to care.

Last night had been magical with Ruby wearing Gabriel's ring and surprising him. Athena didn't think she'd ever forget them in that moment, which led her to thinking about her own parents and how her father had taken care of her mom and the family during the years of her mom's chronic depression. Some things were worth struggling through to keep a marriage and family together.

Ilana arrived next, and after hugging her, Athena spotted Livvy. She practically looked like a teenager in her strappy dress and glittery sandals. The cruise had been the perfect getaway for Livvy and her husband.

When Shannon and Tori arrived, the group was complete. Athena hugged each of them too, marveling how Shannon now seemed comfortable around everyone.

"How are the two newlyweds?" Livvy asked as she walked up to Athena and Tori.

"Great," Athena said, and Tori went into a deep blush.

The other women gathered around, asking Tori about the impromptu marriage.

"When do we get to see the pictures?" Paige asked.

Tori answered that Ilana's husband still needed to load them on her laptop, then everyone could see them.

It took a few moments for everyone to fill their plates from the buffet table at one end of the room—the food Ruby had specially ordered—and take their seats. Once everyone was settled, Athena presented her gifts.

Each woman unwrapped her gift at the same time. After Ruby unwrapped hers, she clapped her hands. "It's gorgeous." She looked up from her crystal statue to Athena, her eyes moist. "This will bring back the most wonderful memories."

"I wanted to thank everyone one last time for coming on this cruise. I'll never forget it," Athena said. "Especially since it included my wedding." The ladies laughed, and Athena looked around the table, her eyes filling with tears. "I feel like each of you has become like a family member to me. Each of you has become very dear to me."

Ruby reached over and patted her hand.

"I know things will be really busy when we return to the States, with all the catching up we'll have to do," Athena continued. Her own to-do list would be huge. "So I wanted to take a couple of moments to ask if we're open to inviting new members into the book club."

"Do you have someone in mind?" Paige asked.

"Yes, but I haven't asked her yet since I wanted to run it by all of you first," Athena said, looking over at Ruby. "But I thought Jackie would love to be a part of the group. Even though she's practically Wonder Woman and has probably read more books than any of us put together, I think she'd appreciate the invitation."

Daisy laughed. "She does kind of remind me of Wonder Woman— even the hair."

They all laughed with Daisy, and then Paige said, "I vote yes."

"We'd love to have her," Ruby said. "I never meant for this group to stop at eight."

The other women agreed, making Athena smile. She owed so much to her book-club friends, and having her sister as a part of the group would be priceless.

"Speaking of books," Ruby said. "Has anyone read anything good while on the cruise?"

Ilana raised her hand, and everyone looked at her. "I, um—I've been doing some research on adoption." Her face flushed as if she was self-conscious.

Shannon, who sat next to her, said, "Does this mean—"

Ilana nodded, a smile brightening her face. "Anyway," she said, her voice trembling a bit with emotion, "the research reminded me about a book I read a couple of years ago called *The Memory Keeper's Daughter*. It's a really touching story."

"I think I've seen some reviews of it," Athena said, which was true for pretty much any book not assigned by the book club. "It was a bestseller, right?"

"I think so. But we could read anything." Ilana looked around, but no one else offered up a book idea.

"I like it," Ruby said. "And let's not wait very long to meet after returning. I know I'll miss you all too much."

"Won't you be busy planning a wedding?" Shannon asked, looking at Ruby from across that table.

Ruby turned bright red. Athena couldn't help but grin. With all the interfering Ruby had done in all of their lives, sweet as it was, the tables had turned.

"It will be a very *small* wedding," Ruby said in a firm voice, but her eyes sparkled. "And . . . nothing will ever be too important to put off book club."

"I'll toast to that," Livvy said, raising her glass of orange juice. All of the other ladies raised their own glasses of water or juice and clinked them together.

Athena tapped her glass against Ruby's, then took a sip of water. "Maybe we should go around and give a quick update on anything we may have missed, since we've all been pulled in different directions."

"What a lovely idea," Ruby said. "Why don't you start, Athena?"

"Of course . . . well, I got married. And I highly recommend it." Everyone chuckled, and Athena looked to Ruby, raising her brows.

"I think everyone knows my big news as well." Ruby held up her hand, showing off the engagement ring.

"We're so happy for you, Aunt Ruby," Shannon said. She glanced about the table and cleared her throat. "I don't have anything that significant to report. I've had a wonderful time, and I think I can safely say I'm very happy my aunt invited me to book club."

"Me too," Ilana said. She fiddled with her fork. "I sort of spilled my big news already, but I do want to say that Ethan is really excited about adopting—which makes me even more excited. At least when I'm not a nervous wreck thinking about everything becoming a new mom will entail."

"You'll be wonderful," Paige said. "I can help you out if you need it."

"Oh, I'll need it!" Ilana said with a laugh.

Paige smiled. "I guess I'll go next. Nothing earth-shattering here, except . . . maybe something good is on the horizon. At least beyond my boys—who are already the best thing in my life."

Livvy said, "Are you referring to what I think you are?"

Athena was surprised to see Paige blush. "Um, yeah. It's pretty much about Derryl. Nothing has happened yet, but I told him that I'm interested in dating him again. He hasn't replied, so . . ." She shrugged and seemed to be trying hard to make light of the silence from Derryl's end.

Everyone broke out into clapping anyway.

Livvy grinned. "That's so exciting." She brushed her hair from her face. "I guess my news is that I've never been more content with my husband. Even looking back on our challenges and our almost-divorce makes me realize that everything has only made our relationship stronger. This cruise and all the wonderful things associated with it have made me realize more than ever what's most important."

"I agree," Daisy said in a soft voice. "In fact, I probably shouldn't confess this because it's so new, but Jared and I . . ." Her voice hitched. "Well, we're going to start dating again. Which sounds pretty crazy. I mean, he's my ex-husband as well as my boyfriend."

"Not so crazy," Tori said. She leaned forward, propping her elbows on the table. "I think when you love someone, you'll pretty much do anything to make it work. Parts of the last year have been absolutely agonizing for me—first, when I had to watch Christopher with all those women on *Vows*, and then when we were finally together to have the media trash everything about us . . . But we're finally married, and that's what's important."

"So true," Livvy said. "Loving someone can be a hard journey at times, but it's also what makes life beautiful."

Athena couldn't agree more. "I feel like I've just read another book—listening to you all for a few minutes has taught me more than I've learned in thirty years on my own."

Ruby smiled at her and slipped an arm around Athena's shoulders. "I think that deserves another toast." Ruby held up her glass, and the other women raised theirs as well. "To all of us—new marriages, old marriages, second chances, great books, and most importantly, friendship."

Chapter 21
PAIGE
FAMILY

THE CRUISE WAS OVER. SOON Paige and her boys would be disembarking, then flying home and returning to their regular lives. Almost no one else in the book club would be returning to *their* regular lives, Paige thought as she zipped her carry-on closed. Everyone else had undergone life-changing events, and she was happy for them all, even if she didn't have hers in front of her. Yet she *was* ready to date Derryl again, to see where that relationship could go. That was, if he was willing to trust her again and give it a try.

But he hadn't texted a word since she'd texted saying she wanted to date again. Not "Good night," not, "That would be great," not even, "Are you out your mind?" She would have preferred rejection to the misery of silence. She had no idea what he was thinking or doing or feeling. Maybe he'd found a hot girlfriend, and Paige's text had been a day late. Maybe . . .

She was half a world away from him and suddenly felt lonely and anxious and moody as she finished her makeup and then finished packing. Her hands shook as she folded Nate's security blanket and slipped it into his backpack, and even though she was trying to make sure they didn't leave anything behind, her mind was really in California. She missed Derryl more than ever, yearned to see his face and hold his hands and feel his lips on hers for the first time in far, far too long.

Would she get that, though, when he hadn't answered her text? She glanced at her phone—yes, it was plugged into its charger, and it wasn't on vibrate. If he'd sent a text, she would have heard it.

Shawn and Nate climbed onto the bed they'd shared for the duration of the cruise and started jumping. For a split second Paige opened her mouth, ready to tell them to stop, but she decided to let it go; they were having fun, and *she* didn't have to straighten the bed afterward. Besides, she had so much nervous energy over her phone that it wouldn't beep that she was tempted to jump beside them.

Instead, she headed to the bathroom for a final check and noted Shawn's toothbrush on the floor. As she picked it up, she heard the ding of a text message.

Paige's eyes popped open. She raced out of the bathroom, handing Shawn his toothbrush as she ran. She stopped by the nightstand but closed her eyes, terrified to look at the phone. The message was probably from Daisy or Ruby; they'd talked about meeting somewhere for one last group picture and to say their good-byes, as some of them had different flights.

It's not from Derryl. Don't get your hopes up.

After taking a deep breath, Paige reached for her phone and opened her eyes. Sure enough, Daisy had sent a text reminding her to meet the group by the gift shop on the fourth level at ten o'clock. Tamping down her disappointment, Paige checked her watch. She and the boys would get there right on time. The ship was due to dock any minute. The group would have plenty of time for final pictures and chitchat. She was rather proud of how quickly she'd gotten herself and the boys ready. After making a final check for their passports, airline tickets, and her ID, she clapped her hands and waved for the boys to come over.

"Time to go, my little men. We're getting off the ship soon."

"And then flying on a plane again?" Shawn asked.

Nate put his arms out like an airplane and buzzed atop the mattress. Paige laughed and called to him again, so he jumped off the bed and "flew" over to her.

"Now get your backpacks," she told them. "Let's go."

The boys put on their packs and trotted behind their mother out the cabin door, down the narrow hall, and to the elevator, where they rode to the fourth floor. As Paige led the way to the gift shop, making sure her boys didn't get lost in the shuffle of other passengers, she again thought through the trip and how amazing everything had turned out for everyone, how in love her friends were. How last night she'd thought she would be entering the same world of love and romance and butterflies in her stomach, of moonlight kisses and holding hands. She'd have given almost anything for even the quiet assurance and safety she'd felt before, having the person she loved an arm's reach away as she slept through the night instead of waking up with worries and staring at the ceiling, alone, at three in the morning.

But maybe she'd spoken too soon. Now she was heading to the gift shop, where everyone would ask how Derryl had replied. She'd have the awful job of admitting that she'd pulled the trigger before he was ready.

And there was the same hollow ache she'd felt all morning. This time her eyes burned with tears too. Paige sniffed and gritted her teeth, determined not to look like she'd been crying when she saw her friends. She'd be happy for them when they said good-byes, and in another day or two she could—hopefully—have a long talk with Derryl that would clarify everything. How she'd last that long she didn't know, but if Derryl hadn't answered by now, there was no reason to think he'd answer before they touched down at LAX.

Paige led her boys to the stairs. *It's okay. Even if things don't work out with Derryl, I know I can handle things on my own. And maybe things can still work out with him. Oh, I hope so.*

She needed a moment to emotionally regroup. When she reached a landing, she pulled her boys to the side.

"What are we doing?" Shawn asked.

Nate looked up expectantly, waiting for the answer to his brother's question.

But Paige wasn't sure what she was doing stopping on a landing in the middle of the ship. What she did know was that for the first time in memory, she didn't really want to see her book-club friends. Not right now, not when they all radiated joy and love, not when they would ask about Derryl and she'd have nothing to tell them. She wasn't sure she could bear public humiliation on top of utter silence from Derryl.

Her phone went off in her pocket, making her startle and her heart about jump out of her chest. Instead of checking it, she just stood there, adrenaline coursing through her body.

But then her rational mind took over. She was probably late, and the ever-punctual Daisy would be wondering where Paige was. Did she have the courage to not show up? No. She couldn't ruin the final group picture. She'd just have to fake a big smile and change the subject— repeatedly, if necessary.

"All right, boys. We're meeting with the book-club ladies one more time for pictures. Let's go," she said, willing her courage to stick around and pasting on a smile.

Nate poked her jeans pocket. "But your phone made a noise. Don't you need to look at it?"

"Oh, right." She'd forgotten that she hadn't actually seen Daisy's text. And she suddenly remembered that the notification hadn't been the one set for most of her contacts. Hand trembling again, Paige reached into her pocket and checked her phone. The text message *wasn't* from Daisy. Or anyone else in the book club.

The chime was Derryl's. The message was from him.

Her heart leapt to her throat, and her thumb hovered over the screen. As soon as she tapped it, she'd know his answer. There would be no going back. She wanted to know—needed to—but at the same time, she couldn't quite get herself to jump off that cliff.

"Here, Mommy," Nate said. "Let me help." And before Paige realized what he was doing, he'd tapped the screen, and Derryl's text appeared.

Miss you. Can't wait to see you.

She stared at the screen for several seconds, the letters growing blurry from the buildup of unshed tears. That was it? He missed her? That was good, right? And he couldn't wait to see her. But he hadn't mentioned a single thing about her last text.

Another possibility dawned on her. Maybe he'd never *gotten* the text. There could have been a sending error—she imagined that international messages had a higher likelihood of delivery problems. Yes. That had to be it. Everything made sense now—Derryl saying he was looking forward to her return. He probably meant it to have the same casual tone he always used, as if she hadn't said a word about dating again.

She found herself able to breathe. She had a clean slate with Derryl. They could have a nice, long talk, face-to-face, when she got home.

No more texting important relationship stuff, she vowed.

So what to say in her reply? Her thumb hovered over the keys as she debated. Before she could decide, another text came through, this one really from Daisy. Paige opened it. As expected, the message asked if she was still coming. Paige quickly typed out a reply.

On our way—almost there!

Now to answer Derryl. If she didn't, he'd worry and wonder, as she had.

Miss you too! See you soon!

She studied the short message and bit her lower lip, debating whether to send it or change it or add to it. But if he hadn't gotten her last text, there was no point in saying more. This was enough. She reread the text three times and then hit send. It would have to do until they saw each other again. She shoved the phone into her pocket, glad she had a friendly, plausible explanation—and something she could tell the book-club ladies when they asked. She no longer wished for a rock to climb under.

She and the boys finally reached the gift shop, where the rest of the book club had already gathered and started taking pictures.

Ruby spotted Paige and clapped. "There she is! Gabriel, you can take the group picture now." She handed Gabriel her camera, kissed his cheek, and scurried to be with the rest of the women.

Paige joined them on one side. Gabriel called to Nate and Shawn and asked for their "help" taking the picture but was really distracting them while their mother was occupied.

Paige smiled through what felt like a hundred photos—everyone had their cameras and camera phones they wanted a photo taken with, and Gabriel spent several minutes juggling them as Paige's cheeks grew tired. At first it was a fake smile brought on by all those leftover nerves from before Derryl's text, but by the end, as she stood there with her best friends, with Daisy's arm around her shoulders, Paige's smile became genuine. She loved these women like family, and she'd remember every moment of this trip with fondness for the rest of her life.

After the pictures, she made sure to give each of the ladies a hug. She'd see them again soon, of course, and she'd likely be in contact with several of them before the next book-club meeting. But she'd never get this moment back, so she savored it.

Soon a voice came over the PA system, in three different languages, saying they could disembark and to please sail with them again.

Paige gathered her boys from Gabriel, who had them enthralled with a magic trick, and then they were off. She and her boys were the last of the group to exit.

Gabriel had his arm around Ruby, and she leaned her head against his shoulder. Daisy and Jared held hands. Tori and Chris sneaked in a kiss or two, as did Athena and Grey. Other passengers jostled and pushed through, until quite a distance grew between Paige and her friends. She kept reminding herself to feel happy for them and to not even think about herself. Not now, except for the brief thought that maybe, just maybe, she could be in a similar position soon.

The walk off the ship felt long, but finally they reached the dock. She looked around, expecting to give her friends a final wave, but she couldn't see any of them. They must have all disappeared into the milling throng so quickly that she'd missed them.

For a second, she felt entirely alone. Her vision became glassy again. She had the urge to pull out her phone and call Derryl right then just to hear his voice. To tell him she wanted another chance and to say so now, before she got on the plane. But she was in the middle of a crowd. Maybe she'd have time to call in a quiet corner of the airport.

She put on her happy voice. "All right, boys. Ready to go? I wonder how many airplanes we'll see."

"Ten!" Nate said. That was as high as he could count; he was still working on keeping his teens in order.

"Twenty-four," Shawn said deliberately, as if he needed to one-up his little brother.

"Only one plane matters to me," a deep voice answered, cutting through the noise of the plaza.

Paige's gaze snapped up. Had she imagined Derryl's voice? She looked left and right, searching the busy port, her heart pounding out of her chest. Of course she'd imagined it. She'd been wishing to talk with Derryl, and this was her mind's way of playing tricks on her. Maybe it was a sign confirming that she should call him before boarding the plane.

But then Paige finally spotted Derryl only a few feet away, right in front of her. He moved closer, and the three people separating them parted, revealing the rest of him—his hair windswept, his jaw sporting the slightest bit of unshaved shadow—the way he looked the most devastatingly handsome. He wore a light-blue button-down shirt and Dockers, and he stood there with his hands in his pockets, his head tilted slightly to one side, his dark sunglasses obscuring his eyes. And he was grinning.

Was it really him? She blinked, not trusting her eyes. But he was real; only that smile would make her this weak in the knees. He took off the sunglasses and tucked them into his shirt pocket, then strolled toward her, closing the distance casually, as if showing up in Rome were completely normal and expected.

He removed one hand from his pocket, revealing his smartphone, which he waved. "Did you mean it?" he asked, stopping only inches from her, so close she could smell his cologne and feel the warmth of his body.

A thousand thoughts spun in her mind, and a cloud of butterflies took flight in her middle. Only one thought mattered. *He did get my text!*

The pieces fell into place: He hadn't replied because in order to be here he must have been on a plane ever since. *This* was his reply.

Yes, she still meant what she'd said; she did want to date him again. Be his girlfriend again. To give it another go.

But not if he didn't really want to.

None of the mess of those jumbled thoughts came out. Instead, she merely nodded. "I meant every word."

Derryl slipped the phone into his pocket, then took her hands in his. "Good. Because I sort of took a gamble and jumped on the first flight I could. This would be really awkward if, you know . . ." His lighthearted tone softened, and he reached forward to brush some hair from Paige's face. At his touch, she closed her eyes, relishing the moment. Oh, how she loved this man. "If you don't feel the same way I do," he finished. "But . . . you do?"

She opened her eyes and looked into the depths of his. Somehow she got her muscles to work and nodded. "Yes," she said. "Assuming you feel the same way you did last February."

Derryl shook his head. "No, I don't." Before her stomach could drop, he went on. "I feel so much *more* than I did then. I love you, Paige. And I'll do whatever it takes, wait as long as it takes, to be with you."

"Mommy?" Nate bounced up and down to get her attention, which she ripped from Derryl's gaze.

She had to clear her throat to speak. "Yeah?"

"Is he going to *kiss* you or something?"

Paige felt a hot blush flame up her cheeks. She looked from Nate to Shawn, who shrugged as if to say, *Whatever, Mom.*

Derryl took a step closer to the boys, then bent down to their eye level. "Would it be all right with you two if I dated your mom?"

Nate put up a chubby hand, giving a thumbs-up. Shawn looked Derryl up and down as if appraising him. "I guess that would be okay—if you're nice to her."

Derryl straightened and slipped an arm around Paige's waist. Her breath caught at his closeness, and her heart melted at his next words. "I promise to be the nicest to her *ever*. I really, really care about your mom. She's pretty amazing, isn't she?"

Both boys nodded emphatically. Derryl went on, this time speaking solemnly and with a perfectly straight face. "If I ever make your mom cry or anything like that, you guys have permission to beat me up."

Shawn's eyes narrowed for a second, and then he stuck out his hand as if striking a bargain. "Deal."

Derryl shook Shawn's hand and then held his hand out for Nate, who followed suit.

"Deal," Nate repeated with a big shake of their hands and a nod to match.

"And now," Derryl said, straightening to face Paige. "I'd really like to kiss you. And then we can change your flight plans so we can all spend some time together."

"But—"

He put a finger to her lips to stop her from speaking. She wanted to kiss that finger. "My treat. Being with you"—he looked at the boys in turn—"and with you, and with you . . . that's what matters."

Nate jumped and clapped his hands. "Like a family? Cool!"

A thrill went through Paige at the word. *Family* was the opposite of alone. Family meant love and happiness . . . and wholeness.

Derryl leaned in and kissed her for the first time in over six months. It wasn't a long kiss, but it was tender and soft and filled with the emotion of their time apart. And it made Paige's toes curl in her shoes. But it was over far too soon.

He pulled back and stroked the top of her hand with his thumb. "What do you think? Should we spend a few days in Rome before we head home?"

"Yeah," she said, looking at him and marveling at how much happiness one woman could feel at once. "I can't imagine anything better." She lifted her heels to reach his lips and kissed him one more time. "As long as we're together."

About Josi

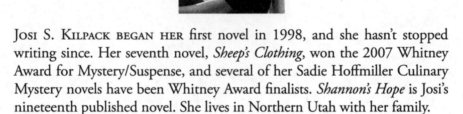

JOSI S. KILPACK BEGAN HER first novel in 1998, and she hasn't stopped writing since. Her seventh novel, *Sheep's Clothing*, won the 2007 Whitney Award for Mystery/Suspense, and several of her Sadie Hoffmiller Culinary Mystery novels have been Whitney Award finalists. *Shannon's Hope* is Josi's nineteenth published novel. She lives in Northern Utah with her family.

For more information about Josi, you can visit her website at www.josiskilpack.com, read her blog at www.josikilpack.blogspot.com, or contact her via e-mail at Kilpack@gmail.com.

About Annette

ANNETTE LYON IS A WHITNEY Award winner, the recipient of Utah's Best of State medal for fiction, and the author of several novels. She loves exploring the power of female friendship in her work. When she's not writing, editing, knitting, or eating chocolate, she can be found mothering and avoiding the spots on the kitchen floor. Visit her online at blog.annettelyon.com and on Twitter: @AnnetteLyon.

About Heather

HEATHER B. MOORE IS THE three-time Best of State and Whitney Award–winning author of several novels. She lives at the base of the Rocky Mountains with her husband, four children, and one black cat. Her favorite holiday is Halloween because she gets to tell fortunes to all of the unfortunate children who dare to visit.

For updates, visit Heather's website, www.hbmoore.com, or blog, http://mywriterslair.blogspot.com. Also visit the Newport Ladies Book Club blog for recipes, sample chapters, and ideas on hosting your own book club: http://thenewportladiesbookclub.blogspot.com.

About Julie

JULIE WRIGHT WAS BORN IN Salt Lake City, Utah. She's lived in LA, Boston, and the literal middle of nowhere (don't ask). She wrote her first book when she was fifteen and has since written sixteen novels—nine of which were traditionally published. Julie won the Whitney Award for Best Romance in 2010 with her novel *Cross My Heart*. She is agented by Sara Crowe at Harvey Klinger, Inc.

She has one husband, three kids, one dog, and a varying number of fish, frogs, and salamanders (depending on attrition).

She loves writing, reading, traveling, speaking at schools, hiking, playing with her kids, and watching her husband make dinner.

She used to speak fluent Swedish but now speaks well enough only to cuss out her children in public settings.

She hates mayonnaise.